THRUWAY DIARIES

Thruway Diaries

Sam Kelley

Library of Congress Control Number:		2012919632
ISBN:	Hardcover	978-1-4797-3279-1
	Softcover	978-1-4797-1011-9
	Ebook	978-1-4797-1012-6

To order additional copies of this book, contact:
Xlibris Corporation
1-888-795-4274
www.Xlibris.com
Orders@Xlibris.com
119187

Additional plays available by Sam Kelley:

Pill Hill

The Blue Vein Society

White Chocolate

Faith, Hope, And Charity: The Story Of Mary McLeod Bethune

To Booker T. and Elnora Kelley and Wesley and Gertrude Kelley, for whom education was not an option but a requirement. Thank you for teaching your descendants to face the struggles of life with dignity and class.

CONTENTS

ACKNOWLEDGMENTS

Racial profiling had reached crisis level for African Americans when I began writing *Thruway Diaries* in the late 1990s. America's War on Drugs practically held Black America hostage, leaving hardly anyone free of the suspicious gaze of zealous law enforcement officials engaged in racial profiling—on foot in the inner city, on the New Jersey Turnpike, or Customs at Chicago's O'Hare International Airport. The ensuing media coverage of the problem sparked serious dialogue and discussion at national and local levels, even resulting in proposed legislation aimed at ending racial profiling. Hopes were raised and optimism was in the air. Then on September 11, 2001, the terrorist attacks occurred, leading to unprecedented national security measures that greatly expanded racial profiling. Further compounding matters has been the racially charged political atmosphere, fueling the immigration debate. This is the atmosphere in which *Thruway Diaries*, initially known as *Driving While Black*, was conceived, written, developed, and brought to life on the stage. Ongoing issues of racial profiling continue to make it relevant today.

I am indebted to the many individuals and artists who have been involved in the development and production of *Thruway Diaries*. A number of theatre companies, college programs, and individuals deserve to be acknowledged, beginning with the African American Theatre workshop class at the State University of New York (SUNY) College at Cortland, and especially Brian Rice for his role as scene and lighting designer. A special thanks to William Lee, Cortland High School drama teacher and adjunct faculty member at Cortland. Bill served as assistant director in the SUNY Cortland production and as one of the police officers for productions at Cortland and with the Paul Robeson Performing Arts Company in Syracuse, New York. The workshop production was first presented in April 2000 as part of the 24th New York State Africana Studies Association Conference (NYASA), which was hosted by SUNY Cortland.

A very special shout-out:

To Dr. Lundeana (Deana) Thomas at the University of Louisville African American Theatre Program and the Juneteenth Theatre Festival for taking on *Thruway Diaries* in its early stages and presenting a staged reading and to Lorna Littleway at Juneteenth Legacy Theatre, which produced a staged reading when it was still titled *Driving While Black* as part of "Lorna Littleway's Juneteenth Jamboree of New Plays" in June 2000. Both Deana and Lorna have presented a number of my works through the years. Thanks also to Professor Annette Grevious at Claflin University for presenting a production in the early stages. Special thanks to the Jubilee Theatre in Fort Worth, Texas, for staging the first full-scale professional production. Sadly, Rudy Eastman, Jubilee artistic director and company co-founder, died unexpectedly the week the production opened. The excellent performances by cast and crew left the playwright and the audience mesmerized.

I must thank the Paul Robeson Performing Arts Company of Syracuse, New York, especially William Rowland II and Annette Adams-Brown, who served as executive artistic director and associate director respectively at the time of this production. The many years in which I was involved with Paul Robeson Performing Arts Company as a playwright, director, actor, and board member have been your gift and your inspiration to me. Working with the outstanding cast and production staff in bringing *Thruway Diaries* to life at Paul Robeson was a playwright's dream. Praise is due to my former student, Victor Garcia, whose rich imagination came to bear in designing the flyers and program cover. Thanks to Jackie Warren-Moore for her insight as co-director, poet, and fellow playwright. Ann Childress proved her mettle as an actress, as an invaluable production staff member, and later as proofreader for the initial draft for the publication, for which I am most grateful.

I must also gratefully acknowledge Renate (Rennie) Simson, Professor and Chair, African American Studies at Syracuse University, who often invites me to her African American Drama class to discuss my work, *Thruway Diaries* in particular. The incisive questions and observations from her students promote a spirited dialogue that continues to inspire and fire my imagination. Indeed, the last visit to her class, and with strong encouragement from Professor Simson, motivated me to move forward with this publication to make the play available to a much wider audience, starting with her own students.

To Judy Shatzky, Bill Lee, Norma McGee, and others, I am indebted to you for taking the time to proofread the play and essay, "And The Beat Goes On: Racial Profiling Before And After 9/11."

Finally, to my dear friend and colleague, Joel Shatzky, thanks for your keen eyes and mind as reader and critic for much of what I have written and produced through the years.

Thruway Diaries

PRODUCTION HISTORY

Thruway Diaries made its professional debut at the Jubilee Theatre in Fort Worth, Texas, on June 4, 2005, with the following artists and production staff:

CAST

Big T	Tyrone King
Naomi	Michele Rene
Little T / Tyrone	Aaron Petite
Josie	Maleka Mahdi
Police Officers	Dennis O'Neill
Police Officers	Jesse Gause
Police Officer Betty	Roblyn Allicia
Police Commissioner	Dennis O'Neill

PRODUCTION AND DESIGN

Director	Rudy Eastman
Managing Director	Benjamin Espino
Musical Director	Joe Rogers
Set Designer	Brynn Bristol
Production Manager	Gloria Abbs
Costumes	Barbara O'Donoghue
Light Design	Jay Isham
Technical Director	Michael Pettigrew
Box Office	Karen Petite

CHARACTERS

BIG T   Late thirties, late seventies
NAOMI   Big T's wife, late thirties, late seventies
LITTLE T / TYRONE   Son/grandson to Big T and
                                       Naomi, late teens, early twenties
JOSIE   Daughter to Big T and Naomi
                                         Age fourteen, late forties

Two male police officers play the following roles:

TAYLOR and BAYLOR   Early fifties, mid-thirties
DIRK and WHELAN   Late twenties, late forties
STRICK and ROCK   Early thirties, early fifties
PENNSYLVANIA STATE TROOPER   Mid-thirties

Additional staff:

POLICE COMMISSIONER   Mid-fifties
BLACK FEMALE POLICE OFFICER   Misfortunes

SETTING

Various locations: Big T's Cadillac. Chicago. Interstate 55. Mississippi. Pennsylvania Interstate 80. Virginia Interstate 95. Virginia jail. Police car. Rest stop picnic area.

TIME

Act One: Early sixties
Act Two: Late 1990s or turn of the century

ACT ONE

Scene One

Early sixties. Chicago. Going home to Mississippi. Rosetta Tharpe's rendition of "Precious Memories" fills the air.

> *Precious memories, unseen angels*
> *Sent from somewhere to my soul*
> *How they linger ever near me*
> *And the sacred past unfold*
>
> *Chorus*
> *Precious memories, how they linger*
> *How they ever flood my soul*
> *In the stillness of the midnight*
> *Precious sacred scenes unfold*

As "Precious Memories" plays, a family photo album begins. The cover is a portrait of Big T and Naomi posing next to a 1963 Eldorado Biarritz (Molly), Big T in tuxedo and Naomi in a fur cape and red evening gown. Flip the page to see Naomi posing next to car alone, reminiscent of a model from Ebony *magazine. Next shot reveals Big T, Naomi, Josie, and Little T seated in car. Additional photos of Big T, Naomi, Josie, and Little T in various poses light up the screen. Dissolve to wedding picture of Naomi and Big T. Naomi is stunning in a red wedding gown, with a white tiara. Several others follow. Music fades to background. Lights rise on Big T snapping picture of Naomi with Polaroid.*

BIG T:	God knows my honey has a patent on red. You know everybody can't wear red.
NAOMI:	(*Flattered.*) Behave yourself, Big T.
BIG T:	*Ebony* magazine couldn't make you look any hotter than you looking right now. Great day in the morning! I have to get a picture of my honey next to her Cadillac. (*As Naomi strikes pose.*) Smile! (*Snapping picture.*) Gotcha! (*Sneaking a smooch.*) Mercy! Baby, how did you know red was my favorite color?
NAOMI:	Mind your business.
BIG T:	You ain't telling me?
NAOMI:	A man isn't supposed to know everything in a woman's head.

Little T enters.

LITTLE T:	How come we always going to Mississippi? I wanna go to New York!
BIG T:	Boy, shut up and get yourself in the car.
LITTLE T:	Don't make sense to buy a spanking brand-new Cadillac just to drive down to the cotton fields. You go to a big city like New York in a brand-new Cadillac.
NAOMI:	(*Warming to the idea of New York.*) Big T, New York doesn't sound so bad.
BIG T:	We're going home to see our kinfolk.
LITTLE T:	They'll be glad to meet us in New York.

Josie enters and flings her arms skyward with a dramatic flair and begins to recite "The Creation" from James Weldon Johnson's God's Trombones, *much to Little T's annoyance.*

JOSIE:

And God stepped out on space,
And he looked around and said,
"I'm lonely—
I'll make me a world."

LITTLE T:	Shut up, girl! Don't you know something else to recite?
JOSIE:	You're jealous because I'm Illinois State Speech Champion!
LITTLE T:	You're state champion because Ruth Ann Mason came down with laryngitis, and nobody else wanted to go in her place.
BIG T:	Get in the car, Little T. You're right behind him, Josie.
LITTLE T:	Do I have to listen to her for eight hours?
BIG T:	I mean for you to get in the car, Little T. (*As Little T slowly gets into car, a teenage sulk spreads across his face.*) Sometimes I think that boy was put on this earth to test my patience.
NAOMI:	(*Teasing.*) He gets it from his daddy.
BIG T:	Woman, if you don't get yourself in this car.
NAOMI:	Big T, maybe we should visit New York or California until things cool down in the South.
BIG T:	You know Mama Bankston is dying to see how her son from Chicago is doing. She ain't gonna be with us always. We got plenty of time to go to New York—California too!

Thomas Dorsey's "Highway to Heaven" fades in for several beats as Big T and family get into Cadillac. Lights dim on Big T and family and rise on Mississippi police officers. They gaze with disdain at proud Big T and family in Cadillac.

BAYLOR:	Chicago niggers.
TAYLOR:	Eldorado Biarritz.
BAYLOR:	Damn agitators.
TAYLOR:	Cut them some slack.
BAYLOR:	Agitators! They're down here to stir up trouble. I'm wiping that damn smile off Sambo's face.
TAYLOR:	Lighten up. Sambo is hustling two jobs to make the payments on that Cadillac. (*Reading license plate.*) "Land of Lincoln."
BAYLOR:	I'll find out if they agitators or not.

Baylor turns on flashing police car lights. Lights rise on Big T and family. Fade on Baylor and Taylor.

BIG T:	Um . . . (*Checking rearview mirror.*) We've got company. (*Noticing Naomi checking speedometer.*) I'm not speeding. I'm cruising in my Cadillac. It ain't no "colored only" section in Big T's Cadillac. (*Watching as Baylor moves in closer.*) Goodness, Naomi. Laurel and Hardy want to play tag.
NAOMI:	Don't make eye contact with them.
BIG T:	I'm staring straight ahead. (*Teasing.*) How about I wink once?
NAOMI:	Big T, don't aggravate them.
BIG T:	I'm driving the speed limit.

Lights rise on Baylor and Taylor.

BAYLOR:	Hey!

Big T stares straight ahead, a mixture of defiance and cautious avoidance.

BIG T:	Hey what?
BAYLOR:	You folk Freedom Riders?
BIG T:	Afraid not.
BAYLOR:	Who the hell are ya?
BIG T:	Proud citizens of these United States of America!
BAYLOR:	Where you *proud* citizens from?
BIG T:	The Windy City!
BAYLOR:	Where the hell is that?
TAYLOR:	Chicago . . .
BIG T:	(*Overlapping Taylor.*) Chicago!
BAYLOR:	What brings you folk to this neck of the woods?
BIG T:	I'm a native Mississippian!
BAYLOR:	Hear the way that uppity nigger talks? (*To Big T.*) Where were you born, boy?
BIG T:	Excuse me?
BAYLOR:	Born, boy! Where the hell were ya born?
BIG T:	Born and raised right here in the Magnolia State.

Lights fade on Big T and family.

BAYLOR:	What I tell ya—agitators. They done forgot our rules of respect.
TAYLOR:	Man sounds like a normal spook to me.
BAYLOR:	You're nuts.
TAYLOR:	I'm nuts now, hey?
BAYLOR:	Let them sit next to us at the lunch counters today, tomorrow we'll be at the back of the bus. Guess where the niggers will be sitting?
TAYLOR:	You're funny, Baylor.
BAYLOR:	They'll be sitting in the front of the bus.
TAYLOR:	Real funny.
BAYLOR:	At the front of the bus, eating fried chicken and chitterlings!
TAYLOR:	You funny as an elephant in a china closet.
BAYLOR:	You won't be laughing when one of them black bucks asks for little Sandy's hand in marriage. Your ass won't be laughing then, buddy.
TAYLOR:	Baylor, old buddy . . .
BAYLOR:	You know what they say?
TAYLOR:	Gotta ask you something.
BAYLOR:	If a nigger whistles at your woman, you gotta lynch the nigger. If you don't, he'll cast his spell.
TAYLOR:	Cast his spell?
BAYLOR:	Hell yeah. Your baby comes out a nigger.
TAYLOR:	I hear that nigger cast a spell on Amber.
BAYLOR:	It ain't funny! This integration mess is like a hungry beast.
TAYLOR:	Yeah?
BAYLOR:	Hell yeah. The more you feed the beast, the bigger that sucker gets, bigger it gets, the more it eats. One day you go out to feed that monster, and it gobbles you up. The beast is chasing us down, partner. We gotta slay that monster. If you don't slay the monster, that sucker will consume your ass for breakfast.
TAYLOR:	Come on . . .
BAYLOR:	You with me or not?

TAYLOR:	Baylor . . .
BAYLOR:	Hey—you with me or not?

Lights fade on Baylor as Taylor stares at him uneasily. Lights rise on Big T and family.

NAOMI:	Big T, these people don't have the fear of God in them.
BIG T:	They don't have to fear God. They are God.
NAOMI:	You know where they found Waddell and Langston.
BIG T:	Yeah, I know what they did to them.
NAOMI:	I don't want bulldozers digging me up out here.
LITTLE T:	See? I told you to go to New York.
JOSIE:	I want to go to California.
LITTLE T:	Shut your trap, girl!
BIG T:	Mind your business, Little T. I'm proud to be an American. You know what I told that Cadillac dealer? I said to him, "Mister, I want a ride that's gonna make my wife feel like a queen." You got something against feeling like a queen?
NAOMI:	I don't want to be a dead and buried queen.
BIG T:	Most colored women get to be a queen on their wedding day. Next day, it's back to the white woman's kitchen cooking and washing dishes.
JOSIE:	I'm not working in no white woman's kitchen.
NAOMI:	Josie . . .
JOSIE:	I'm not!
LITTLE T:	Shut up, girl!
BIG T:	Mind your business, boy. As for you, Josie, you don't know what you'll end up doing. Your mama would be cleaning and cooking for Doug Winston right now if she hadn't come to her senses and moved to Chicago to be with me.
NAOMI:	Let it rest, Big T.
LITTLE T:	You never told us you cooked and cleaned for white folks.
NAOMI:	I have never cleaned or cooked for white folks a day in my life. I cooked and cleaned for myself. The

people in whose employ I worked happened to be white. That's all I have to say about it. Period!

BIG T: Look at my own sister, Teresa? She stayed behind to work for Edgar Raleigh. Where has that got her? Five mulatto babies in ten years, and she is still going in every day to work for him. Just like nothing happened. Don't tell me Madam Raleigh doesn't know where Massa Raleigh is going fishing.

NAOMI: That's enough, Big T.

BIG T: I know you ain't talking to me. Not after I sent my baby sister three train tickets to get her out of that white woman's kitchen. I drove down here four years straight to get her up myself. "Come back this time next year. God is my witness. I'm going back to Chicago with you." "Naw, woman, you're going back now." "I just need to save up a little more money." I come back. She greets me with a big belly—ready to deliver another Raleigh baby. It's a wonder Raleigh's crazy wife ain't burned her alive.

NAOMI: (*Agitated.*) Stop it!

BIG T: Okay, okay, I'm washing my hands of the whole darn business. (*Checking out rearview mirror, uneasily.*) Jesus, baby, them fools are right back on our tail.

NAOMI: We should have gone no farther than St. Louis.

BIG T: Told ya, Mama gotta see how her Chicago son is doing.

NAOMI: She could meet us in St. Louis.

BIG T: Goodness. What's on their minds now?

NAOMI: Don't provoke them, Big T.

BIG T: I'm staring at the road, Naomi.

NAOMI: These white folk ain't been the same since that Montgomery woman refused to give up her seat on that bus.

JOSIE: Her name is Rosa Parks.

NAOMI: You know they're angry as the devil over this integration business.

BIG T: It's time Negroes stand up and be counted.

LITTLE T:	I don't want to die being counted.
BIG T:	Shut your mouth, boy.
LITTLE T:	Well, I don't!
BIG T:	I mean it, Little T!
JOSIE:	Dad, can I sit between you and Mom?
NAOMI:	Stay put, Josie. Stare straight ahead. Don't make eye contact.
NAOMI:	God, help us.

Lights fade on Big T and family and rise on Baylor.

BAYLOR:	How much is that Cadillac worth?
TAYLOR:	It's fresh off the sales floor.
BAYLOR:	What you think the parts will bring?
TAYLOR:	Ask Wayne.
BAYLOR:	Wayne Bingham is gonna cut that Eldorado up like country fried chicken.
TAYLOR:	What about the wife and the kids?
BAYLOR:	Letting them go. We're keeping the black buck with the car.
TAYLOR:	I don't want another Jimmy Wiggins on our hands.
BAYLOR:	You forget?
TAYLOR:	Forget what?
BAYLOR:	Wayne's body shop is on the river? He's got concrete slab. We'll sink that nigger in the river quick as nothing.
TAYLOR:	You got a mother and two kids to get rid of.
BAYLOR:	Didn't you hear me say we let the wife and kids go?
TAYLOR:	Four bodies is a lot of digging if something goes wrong.
BAYLOR:	Don't go limp on me, okay, partner?
TAYLOR:	I ain't gonna be around when the FBI digs up another Jimmy Wiggins.
BAYLOR:	I'm taking charge of this one myself.
TAYLOR:	Damn you, Baylor. Get over Amber.
BAYLOR:	You telling me what I gotta get over?

TAYLOR:	That nigger didn't force her to run off to Los Angeles with him.
BAYLOR:	Screw you, sissy! (*As lights rise on Big T and family.*) Hey, boy?
BIG T:	Hey what?
BAYLOR:	Pull off on that dirt road up yonder.
BIG T:	At your service!

Big T pulls off road behind Baylor.

NAOMI:	Why are we leaving the highway?
BIG T:	Didn't you hear the man say pull off at the next road? What I'm gonna do? Keep driving? I ain't broke no law.
LITTLE T:	You're a colored man in a Cadillac. That's a crime.
BIG T:	Quiet, boy.
LITTLE T:	I knew it!
BIG T:	Knew what?
LITTLE:	We should have gotten a doo doo brown Impala.
BIG T:	Willie Peterson got four tickets down here last month in his doo doo brown Impala. Four tickets!
NAOMI:	Lord, have mercy.
BIG T:	Would have gotten six if he hadn't paid off the police in Illinois and Missouri.
JOSIE:	We should have taken the plane.
LITTLE T:	What airport you landing at?
JOSIE:	Memphis.
LITTLE T:	You might as well drive.
BIG T:	Next time we come down here, you folk catching the train and riding in the colored section with the fried-chicken-eating Negroes.
LITTLE T:	We got money to pay off the cops?
NAOMI:	Behave, Little T.
JOSIE:	Back my poem! "The children of Israel lost hope . . ."
LITTLE T:	Shut up, girl!
JOSIE:	Daddy!
LITTLE T:	You've been reciting *God's Trombones* all the way from Chicago.

| BIG T: | Little T, I ain't asking you no more, okay? Carry on, Josie. |

Josie's eyes grow wide with unease.

JOSIE:

> *The children of Israel all lost hope;*
> *And they mumbled and grumbled among themselves:*
> *Were there no graves in Egypt?*
> *And they wailed aloud to Moses and said:*
> *Slavery in Egypt was better than to come*
> *To die here in this wilderness.*

A worried Naomi shouts out to Big T.

NAOMI:	Big T! We've gone past the last house.
LITTLE T:	Dad, where we going?
JOSIE:	We're headed for the woods!
NAOMI:	Stop the car!
BIG T:	I can't stop, Naomi!
NAOMI:	I said stop the car! Turn around and get out now!
LITTLE T:	Head back out to the highway.
BIG T:	And let them fools shoot up my Cadillac?
LITTLE T:	Better they shoot this car than me!
BIG T:	Shut your damn mouth!
NAOMI:	If something happens to us, I want it to be next to the highway.
LITTLE T:	We'll have witnesses!
NAOMI:	Go on, Big T! Get out of here!
BIG T:	Okay, okay, I'm turning around. Everybody hold tight.
JOSIE:	(*Shrieking in terror.*) Dad, he's cutting us off!
BIG T:	Quiet down, Josie! (*Trying to collect himself.*) Everybody calm down—calm down, okay? I'm in charge here.

Baylor takes his sadistic nature in stride. Taylor, younger, laid back, has the John Wayne act down pat. Taylor pulls shotgun from trunk.

BAYLOR:	Boy, where you get this here car?
BIG T:	Bought it.
BAYLOR:	Whatcha buy it wid?
BIG T:	My money.
BAYLOR:	Got us a smart-ass Chicago nigger on our hands.
TAYLOR:	Where you folk headed?
BIG T:	Smithville.
TAYLOR:	What brought you through Barksdale?
BIG T:	Gassing up.
BAYLOR:	Bull. You been running all over town in this car.
BIG T:	I beg your pardon?
BAYLOR:	Down here to stir up trouble are ya, boy?
BIG T:	Nope, won't be no trouble from me if you guys don't make any.
BAYLOR:	Boy, did I hear you say "no sir"?
BIG T:	I don't remember.
BAYLOR:	You don't say. Get out the car. I'm gonna refresh your memory. Get your ass out the car, nigger!

Big T gets out of the car. A stoic posture hardly camouflages his unease in this moment of fearful uncertainty.

BAYLOR:	Over in front of the headlights. Fine-looking car you got.
BIG T:	Thank you.
BAYLOR:	We got us a problem.
BIG T:	Problem?
BAYLOR:	Looks to me like your headlights need cleaning. (*As Big T hesitates.*) I said it looks to me like the headlights need cleaning.
NAOMI:	Big T . . .
BIG T:	Calm down, baby. Everything's gonna be all right.
TAYLOR:	Hey. I wouldn't take too long if I was you.
BAYLOR:	On your damn knees, boy. On your knees, nigger! (*Big T gets down on his knees.*) Clean off them headlights. (*Big T reaches for handkerchief.*) Halt! Touch 'em wid ya hands, and I'm gonna splatter your colored brains from here to Chicago. Start licking, boy. (*Big T starts licking. Naomi closes her eyes*

	in prayer.) You taking all day on them headlights? Boy, I'm wiping them headlights with my hankie when you done licking. I pick up one gnat turd, and you're licking the whole goddamn Cadillac.
JOSIE:	(*Crawling into front seat with Naomi.*) Mom . . .
NAOMI:	Pray to God, children, with all your might.
LITTLE T:	There is no god in Mississippi.
NAOMI:	Little T! Start praying—now!
LITTLE T:	What you gonna do? Tell Dad? Look where he is? (*Naomi shoots Little T a look to kill.*) Okay, okay. I'm praying.

Big T gets up. He starts to spit.

| | |
| **BAYLOR:** | Hey! No spitting. (*Big T forces down dirt, grime, and bugs in painful swallow. He starts to walk back to car.*) Where the hell you think you're going? You forgot the other side. (*Big T turns to Baylor.*) Boy, look me in the eye one more time, and I'll strike you blind. (*Noticing Big T is still standing.*) Start licking, nigger! |

Little T threatens to get out the car. Taylor thrusts the butt of his rifle against the ground. Naomi pulls Little T back into car.

| | |
| **BIG T:** | (*With a protective scold.*) Stay put, son. |

Big T glances around at his family. Then kneels, calmly, and licks.

NAOMI:	Memorize the license plate.
JOSIE:	I already did.
NAOMI:	When they get close, get their badge numbers.
LITTLE T:	Lots of good that's gonna do.
NAOMI:	Quiet, Little T.
BAYLOR:	I'm calling the wife and kids out to give you a hand if you ain't wrapped up in sixty seconds. (*Big T licks faster.*) There's gnat shit over in the corner. Get to licking. Gnat shit is still there. (*Big T licks more. He*

gets up and starts back to the car.) Where the hell you think you're going?

BIG T: (*Folding his arms in silent defiance.*) To my car.

BAYLOR: Unfold your arms, boy. (*Big T places hands in pocket.*) Take your hands out your pocket. (*Big T starts to car.*) Hey! Did I give you permission to go to your car?

BIG T: No, sir.

BAYLOR: Drop your pants. (*Big T doesn't move.*) Drop your goddamn pants, nigger!

Big T hesitates. Taylor reaches in car and places hand on Naomi's shoulder. Big T starts after him. Taylor slams gun against car.

NAOMI: Stop, Big T!

Big T stops.

TAYLOR: Love the wife and the kids, do ya?

NAOMI: Big T . . . I'm okay.

Big T slowly removes his pants. Baylor pulls Big T's wallet from his pocket, takes the money, and throws wallet at Big T's feet. Baylor keeps pants.

BAYLOR: I'm getting your keys.

Baylor pulls the keys from the ignition. Big T picks up wallet and starts to walk to his car.

TAYLOR: Any contraband?

BIG T: No, sir.

TAYLOR: Bootleg liquor?

BIG T: No, sir.

TAYLOR: Illegal drugs?

BIG T: No, sir.

TAYLOR: Counterfeit money?

BIG T: I'm clean, mister.

TAYLOR: What's in your trunk?

BAYLOR: (*Pulling suitcase from trunk.*) I'm checking.

NAOMI:	(*Jumping out of car, in fury.*) Don't you dare put your filthy hands on my clothes!
BIG T:	Naomi, get back in the car.
NAOMI:	You are not looking for contraband!
BIG T:	Get back in the car, Naomi.
TAYLOR:	Best you obey your husband, ma'am.
BIG T:	Naomi, please.
NAOMI:	Put your paws on a single garment in my suitcase, I'll burn every last one of them. (*Turning to Taylor.*) Sir, I beg you, stop your partner.
TAYLOR:	Hold on a minute, Baylor. (*Pulling suitcase from Baylor's hand, zipping suitcase back up.*) Feels like clothes to me.
BAYLOR:	You sure about that, partner?
TAYLOR:	Sure as shit stinks.
BAYLOR:	I'm having a look for myself. (*Pulling out women's belongings.*) They look pretty expensive to me. (*Closing suitcase.*) Boy, don't let sunup catch your black ass in Mississippi.

Naomi takes suitcase and heads to police car.

TAYLOR:	Hey, miss!
BAYLOR:	Where you think you going?
BIG T:	Naomi!
NAOMI:	(*Placing suitcase in police car.*) You can donate these to the needy.
BIG T:	Naomi.
BAYLOR:	Well now. (*Pulling Big T's suitcase from car and throwing it in police car.*) Wouldn't be fair for me to take only the lady's suitcase, would it now?
TAYLOR:	You folk have a pleasant trip.
NAOMI:	We'll do our best.

Lights fade on police car.

BIG T:	What the hell you do that for? Those clothes cost an arm and a leg. (*Naomi starts for car, quietly cringing*

and brushing at her dress.) Don't walk away from me when I'm talking to you.

NAOMI: I'm getting in the car, Big T.

BIG T: Not until I'm done speaking. Next time I tell you to get in the car you get in the damn car.

NAOMI: Who is to say Josie and I weren't next?

BIG T: You will not disobey me in front of white folk.

NAOMI: Do you think it mattered one bit to them?

BIG T: Get in the car.

Naomi gets into car. Big T cranks up.

NAOMI: Where do you think you're going?

BIG T: To get some pants to cover my black behind.

NAOMI: No, you're not.

BIG T: Yes, I am. (*As Naomi gets out of the car.*) What are you doing?

NAOMI: You aren't moving this car one inch until you apologize to me.

BIG T: We've got to get out of here before those fools come back and kill us all. Didn't you hear that man say don't let sunup catch us down here?

NAOMI: I don't care what that man said.

Walking away from car to get out of earshot of Josie and Little T, with Big T following.

BIG T: What's the matter with you?

NAOMI: I didn't quit Doug Winston's household because I was tired of cooking and cleaning for white folk.

BIG T: What the hell does Doug Winston have to do with us?

NAOMI: I ran away, Big T, I ran all the way to Chicago.

BIG T: What are you talking about?

NAOMI: You're not deaf.

BIG T: (*Halting.*) You're not saying . . .

NAOMI: Yes, I'm saying it. I ran away because he couldn't keep his hands off me. (*Big T is stunned.*) I ran all the way to Chicago. I'm still running. Do you ever wonder why I wore red for our wedding? I was tainted, stained. (*Moving few more steps away from car.*) I wash and scrub until my skin is raw, and I still smell Doug Winston on me. When that policeman reached for my bags, I smelled Doug Winston all over. (*Fighting back tears.*) I'm sorry, Big T. I'm sorry.

Big T collects himself.

BIG T:	Naomi . . .
NAOMI:	Please . . . Don't make me tell you the rest of it.
BIG T:	You want me to . . .
NAOMI:	Kill a white man in Mississippi? Are you crazy? You and every colored man down here will be bait for the lynch mob. Get in the car, and don't look back.

Big T opens door. Naomi climbs in on driver's side, staying close.

LITTLE T:	Hey, Dad. (*Throwing pants to Big T.*) Mine will fit you okay.
BIG T:	(*Throwing pants back to Little T.*) Keep your pants on, son.
LITTLE T:	I see you're too big for my britches.
BIG T:	How much you think we can get for this Eldorado?
NAOMI:	We're not selling my car.
BIG T:	I'm parking this piece of trash in Chicago, and I'm never setting foot in it again.
NAOMI:	I'm not feeling like a queen today, but I might be Queen Naomi when I wake up tomorrow morning.
BIG T:	Can you feel like a queen in a doo doo brown Impala?
NAOMI:	It's not the Cadillac you hate.
LITTLE T:	I'll drive it. Time for me to get my license.
BIG T:	Quiet, boy. Josie, go on with your poem.
JOSIE:	Mama . . . Who is Doug Winston?

BIG T:	That's grown folks talk, Josie. Let me hear your poem.
JOSIE:	(*Hurt, quietly stubborn.*) I forgot it.
BIG T:	Josie?

Josie sits stubbornly mum. Little T begins to recite the poem in an innocent attempt to break the painful stalemate.

LITTLE T:	*And Moses lifted his rod* *Over the Red Sea . . .*
JOSIE:	Daddy, make him stop reciting my poem!
LITTLE T:	You forgot it.
BIG T:	Little T, until we get home to Chicago, James Weldon Johnson belongs to Josie.
LITTLE T:	Mrs. Simms, my literature teacher, she says James Weldon Johnson belongs to all people—black, white, red, and yellow. His message is universal. I can recite him if I want to.
BIG T:	You can recite it from the trunk of my Cadillac. Go on with your poem, Josie.
JOSIE:	Mama?
NAOMI:	Yes, dear?
JOSIE:	Did Doug Winston do something to you?

Big T places his arm, protectively, around Naomi. She reaches her hand, palm upward, over her shoulder toward Josie, who leans forward and clasps her mother's hand.

NAOMI:	Mama is going to help you with your poem. Okay, baby? *But Moses said:* *Stand still! Stand still!* *And see the Lord's salvation.* *For the God of Israel* *Will not forsake his people.*
JOSIE:	Okay, Mom. (*Speaking with difficulty*) I got it. *And Moses lifted up his rod* *Over the Red Sea;*

And God with a blast of his nostrils
Blew the waters apart,
And the children of Israel all crossed over
On to the other side.

Lights fade on Big T and family as Josie recites and Big T drives on. "Precious Memories" fades in.

Scene Two

Chicago. Morning. Late nineties. Portrait of Big T and Naomi gives way to Tyrone standing next to Cadillac in dreadlocks. Tupac Shakur blares as "Precious Memories" fades out. Lights up. Tyrone, a young black male in dreads and Jamaican-style knitted cap, is sitting in car. The Eldorado has been modernized, but the classic design remains. Two policemen, Whelan and Dirk, rush forward.

WHELAN:	Out the car, boy, out the car now!
TYRONE:	(*In no hurry.*) I'm getting out.
WHELAN:	Move it!
TYRONE:	I am moving!
WHELAN:	Shut the hell up!
TYRONE:	Man!

Whelan shoves his hand into Tyrone's chest as if to check his pulse to put fear into his heart. He searches him with brute physicality. Then he checks out car.

WHELAN:	We know what you do for a living.
DIRK:	Automatic air.
WHELAN:	Ain't *we* cool!
DIRK:	Leather!
WHELAN:	Pressing ass in high comfort.
DIRK:	Power windows!
WHELAN:	Living the high life.
DIRK:	Check this out, partner.
WHELAN:	What you got?
DIRK:	Only seven thousand miles on this ride.
WHELAN:	Fan my lily white ass with a colored brick.

DIRK:	Start talking, boy.
TYRONE:	Granddad kept it on the blocks.
WHELAN:	You making me out a liar?
DIRK:	Color TV . . .
WHELAN:	We gotta watch BET and MTV, don't we now?
DIRK:	Sunroof!
WHELAN:	That how you got that Nairobi tan?
TYRONE:	Look, man . . .
WHELAN:	You look, boy!
DIRK:	Cruise control. CD, DVD, TV . . .
WHELAN:	Dammit, partner! Quit drooling over this pimpmobile. Check BCI. (*Dirk heads off stage.*) Hey, Superfly.
TYRONE:	Man . . .
WHELAN:	I ain't asking you how many whores (*pronounced hos*) you got on the street.
TYRONE:	I don't have any whores on the street.
WHELAN:	Hands back on the car! No whores on the street?
TYRONE:	Naw, man.
WHELAN:	How much did they hit you up to customize this pimpmobile?
TYRONE:	Fifty-two hundred.
WHELAN:	You gonna tell me whose car this is?
TYRONE:	I told you already. This is Grandpa T's car.
WHELAN:	Where you say you coming from, boy?
TYRONE:	Detroit.
WHELAN:	Making a drop?
TYRONE:	I'm an automotive design student at Michigan University.
WHELAN:	Yeah, and I'm Prince and Tupac rolled into one.
TYRONE:	I modernized this car as my senior thesis.
WHELAN:	You flunked.
TYRONE:	What!
WHELAN:	Flunked, you flunked, boy!
TYRONE:	What do you mean I flunked? I got an A.
WHELAN:	You get an F. No hot tub, no wet bar—you flunked.
TYRONE:	Listen man . . .
WHELAN:	You listen . . .

TYRONE:	I'm not a dealer . . .
WHELAN:	*He's not a dealer!*
TYRONE:	And I'm not a user!
WHELAN:	*A black guy who doesn't do crack!*
TYRONE:	I don't.
WHELAN:	Hey, you don't deal. You don't snort. You got no whores on the street. So open the trunk of that Cadillac and prove it to me.
TYRONE:	You got a search warrant?
WHELAN:	What did you ask me?
TYRONE:	Search warrant, you got a search warrant?
WHELAN:	How about I hold you in Cook County Jail until I get you one? Your jail buddies will gladly *search* you.
DIRK:	The car checks out. It's registered to a Tyrone Bankston.
WHELAN:	Hey, I'm keeping my eyes on you, kid.
DIRK:	Hey, kid, minor case of mistaken identity.

Whelan and Dirk head off.

WHELAN:	Boy, did we put the fear of God in that spook's ass.

Lights fade as Tyrone climbs back into car, more annoyed than angry. Lights rise on photo of a beaming Big T and Naomi in contemporary dress next to updated Cadillac. Big T and Naomi are now in their seventies, well preserved. The golden years have been good to them.

BIG T:	(*Offstage.*) Tyrone should have been here by now.
NAOMI:	(*Offstage.*) Pray to God nothing happened to the child.
BIG T:	(*Offstage.*) He'd have called by now if something happened to him.
NAOMI:	(*Offstage.*) Careful with Denise's dress.
BIG T:	(*Offstage.*) I ain't touched the dress yet, Naomi.
NAOMI:	(*Offstage.*) I'm telling you before you touch it.

Sound of car horn is heard.

BIG T:	(*Offstage.*) I hear that Cadillac. Let's get moving.

Lights fade on photos.

Scene Three

Chicago. Few minutes later. Lights rise as Big T and Tyrone load the Cadillac. An anxious Naomi directs. Big T is at the end of his patience.

NAOMI:	My wedding outfit goes in first.
BIG T:	I'm putting it in first, sweetheart.
NAOMI:	Keep the bag straight.
BIG T:	I'm keeping the bag straight as an arrow. That good enough, Naomi?
NAOMI:	Fine. Now, Denise's wedding dress goes on top of my outfit.
BIG T:	Nowhere else for her dress to go.
NAOMI:	I don't want a blemish on it, T Baby! Not one blemish!
BIG T:	I told you to ship this dress to Virginia.
NAOMI:	You're talking out of your head.
BIG T:	No such thing.
NAOMI:	Ship my granddaughter's wedding dress to Virginia? You most certainly are talking out of your head.
BIG T:	It'll be waiting on us when we get there. Tell your grandma, Tyrone.
NAOMI:	Keep your mouth shut, Tyrone. The salesman at Neiman Marcus quoted me $12,000 for this dress.
TYRONE:	Twelve thousand dollars for a wedding dress?
NAOMI:	God and Big T are my witnesses. I kept going back until I got the design in my head. Guess what I did then, Tyrone?
BIG T:	Drove me crazy is what she did.
NAOMI:	I went home, and I stitched it for nine thousand dollars less than Mr. Galvano was asking. This is a Naomi Louise Bankston special!

BIG T: Tyrone, your grandma dragged me to every wedding salon in Chicago looking for that darn dress. Did she tell you how much the materials cost?

NAOMI: Fifty dollars a yard!

TYRONE: Fifty dollars a yard! Grandma? Can I have a peek?

NAOMI: You know better!

TYRONE: I'm not the groom. I'm the bride's brother.

NAOMI: You're in the wedding party.

BIG T: If it helps you any, Tyrone, it's a white dress with some beads covering it.

NAOMI: It's not just white, T Baby, it is stark white. Stark white goes perfect with Denise's ebony skin. We have to make sure no dirt gets on it. If a single speck of dirt gets on it, everybody in the chapel will be whispering. "Look, the child's got dirt on her dress. Poor thing, she's starting her life with stains on her marriage!"

BIG T: (*Opening car door.*) Naomi, if you don't get yourself in the car—

NAOMI: It's the truth, T Baby. Can't nobody on God's earth out talk our folk in the gossip department.

BIG T: Now, you know what I've been putting up with for fifty years. (*Calling for Josie.*) Josie! It's time to get on the road. Tyrone, get your mama.

TYRONE: You get her. She won't listen to me.

BIG T: You have to ask first.

TYRONE: I'm telling you.

BIG T: Josie!

TYRONE: Mom! You're holding up the ride!

JOSIE: (*Offstage.*) I'm not deaf, Tyrone!

TYRONE: What I tell you!

BIG T: The sun is halfway to Los Angeles, and we're still in Chicago!

TYRONE: Mom!

JOSIE: I'm coming! I'm coming! Don't rush me.

TYRONE: I'm not rushing you!

Josie enters with arm full of books.

JOSIE:	I've been dressed since seven this morning. I'm bringing plenty of reading to keep me company.
BIG T:	Please, Josie, I hope you aren't going to read aloud to us all the way to Virginia.
JOSIE:	I am reading to myself.
BIG T:	Good. I'll be bored to hell and back.
JOSIE:	You can smooch in the back seat with Mama.
TYRONE:	Dinosaurs don't smooch.
JOSIE:	Tyrone! I know you did not call your grandparents dinosaurs.
TYRONE:	They too old for that smooching stuff.
BIG T:	Now that's where you're wrong, young fellow. Your grandma and me can do anything you and your gal do. Only difference now is it takes us all night to do what we used to do all night long.
NAOMI:	T. Baby, stop congratulating yourself.
BIG T:	Wouldn't take but a few hot minutes if you'd let me do my Viagra thing.
TYRONE:	Granddad!
JOSIE:	Oh no! He did not say Viagra!
NAOMI:	Oh yes, he did, child!
BIG T:	My honey rations out the tango every full moon. And I got to howl like a wolf before she knows I'm aching to do the mating dance.
NAOMI:	You aren't bringing that Viagra mess into our house. Spice up your cocoa with a little cinnamon and fresh ginger and you'll be all tuned up.
BIG T:	I'm tired of sipping hot cocoa every night. Got to get up at two o'clock every morning to empty my bladder.
NAOMI:	That's because you drink it down too fast. You're supposed to sip it, T Baby.
BIG T:	Sip it, drink it, gulp it, it's going down the toilet at 2:00 am.
JOSIE:	Excuse me, may we bless this trip before you two start to tango. Lord, we ask your blessings for a safe and pleasant journey every mile of the way. Amen.

Naomi, Big T and Tyrone follow: "Amen!"

BIG T:	Mercy, Josie! What you do, join the United Methodists? That prayer ain't long as a roach turd.
JOSIE:	Yes, as a matter of fact, I am now a United Methodist.
BIG T:	Traitor!
JOSIE:	Excuse me?
BIG T:	I knew it.
JOSIE:	I still got my Baptist spunk if that's what you're worried about.
BIG T:	Then how come you deserted your Baptist roots?
JOSIE:	I like having my Sunday afternoons off.
BIG T:	Well now, it ain't exactly my business, but if you don't mind my asking—
JOSIE:	About what I do with my Sunday afternoons? I cuddle up with the latest best-selling novel and a glass of my favorite Chardonnay.
BIG T:	You cuddling up with a bottle of wine. You need to cuddle up with a man.
JOSIE:	Mama, shut your husband up.
NAOMI:	Behave yourself, T Baby.
BIG T:	A strong, healthy woman like Josie needs a real man who can tango with her until she shouts like a holy roller.
JOSIE:	Shut him up, Mama!
NAOMI:	T Baby, I'd hate to have you riding in the trunk.
BIG T:	Forget that hot chocolate. We're going way down to Jamaica and help my honey get her groove back.
JOSIE:	Mama won't need you when she gets to Jamaica. Not with all that hot chocolate stalking the beaches.
NAOMI:	Tell him, child! My Jamaica man gonna have two strong arms to cuddle me while I sip rum and strawberry daiquiris.
BIG T:	I got your Jamaica stud beat by a Texas mile. I got two strong arms and *three* hot legs to keep you warm.
NAOMI:	Yeah, but I can't count on but two of your legs working on your best day. And don't let it rain! Nooooo Lord!
JOSIE:	Somebody bring on the liniment!

NAOMI:	Child, when it rains, I can't count on a single one of his legs working.
JOSIE:	Hold the liniment. Roll out the wheelchair!
BIG T:	Tyrone!
TYRONE:	Yes, sir?
BIG T:	Son, don't just sit there like a knot on a log. You hear these women putting my business in the street.
TYRONE:	What I'm supposed to do?
BIG T:	You ain't one bit of help to your granddad.
NAOMI:	You're doing just fine, Tyrone.
BIG T:	Tyrone is too head over heels in love with Heather to think about his Granddad. God only knows why he ain't come home with himself a professor on his arm.
NAOMI:	What is Tyrone gonna do with a professor?
BIG T:	Don't you remember what happened to Willie Bee Yancy? That man sent his daughter way up north to college—almost to Canada, to one of them big expensive Ivy League colleges.
TYRONE:	Dartmouth.
BIG T:	Dartmouth! That gal was writing back home, talking about how much she was head over heels for Shakespeare and Walt Whitman and Ralph Waldo Emerson, all them famous dead white men. Next thing Willie Bee knows, Vivian comes riding up to the door with the literature professor on her arm. White guy!
NAOMI:	Now, you know that was love blessed by God.
BIG T:	Had to be, 'cause them Mississippi cops would a buried both of them and not breathed a word about it. Well, anyway, this professor and Vivian, they want to get married. The professor was standing there, grinning like a monkey in heat, telling Willie Bee that Vivian was the best student he ever had. Willie Bee looks at the professor with that Mississippi curiosity. "Well now, professor, how many of your students have you *had?*" "Oh no, sir, I didn't mean it like that. I meant she's the smartest student I every taught." Willie Bee goes,

	"Well now, what were you *teaching* my Vivian? She said she was in love with Shakespeare? You don't look like Shakespeare to me. Looks to me like you teaching her a whole lot of stuff that ain't written in the books."
NAOMI:	Ain't that the truth!
BIG T:	Willie Bee gave them his blessing. They moved to California, and he got a good job at that big hippie university.
TYRONE:	Berkeley.
BIG T:	University of California at Berkeley! Vivian got her PhD, and they raised four kids. You know they still together. Now that's old fashion love. Matter of fact, they the only folk in California I know who ain't got divorced.
JOSIE:	Dad, please! There are plenty of married people in California.
BIG T:	I said the only folk in California *I* know who ain't got divorced. Some California folk out there been married one, two, three, four five, six, seven, eight, a dozen times!
JOSIE:	Do you mind?
BIG T:	I'm done with it. As I was saying . . . What was I saying before I was so rudely interrupted? Goodness, I'm having one of them old folks' moments.
TYRONE:	You mean senior moment.
BIG T:	Naomi has senior moments. I have old folks' moments.
NAOMI:	T Baby, dear? It's time for your nap.
BIG T:	Mercy! Y`all hear how sweet my honey bun tells me to shut the hell up? "T Baby, dear? It's time for your nap."
NAOMI:	Tyrone, let your granddad sleep as long as he wants. When he starts to snore, I'm gonna clap my hands to make him stop. Been doing it for fifty years. It's my secret to a good night's sleep.
BIG T:	When my honey starts to snore, I snap my finger.
NAOMI:	I don't snore.

BIG T:	Woman, you snore loud enough to scare the snout off a razorback hog.
NAOMI:	You sure about that, T Baby?

Big T places arm around Naomi.

BIG T:	I say we call a few hogs together.

Lights fade on family car. "Highway to Heaven" fades in. Lights rise on police commissioner as music fades out.

Scene Four

Afternoon. Police commissioner at press conference.

POLICE COMMISSIONER: What? Absolutely not. We do not engage in racial profiling. No, absolutely not! That's absurd. Yes. I said absurd. It's absurd for any of you people here to think that our guys would systematically engage in racial profiling. Race is not a consideration in any shape or form in our stops and searches. My officer stops a vehicle, not a colored—I mean Negro, excuse me, black person. If the driver happens to be black, so be it. Nope. We don't go looking for a colored—excuse me, black guy. We call the shots as we see them. Let me put it this way. Race—I mean color, or ethnicity—is one of many factors taken into account when our officers stop a driver. If I see a colored guy in a white neighborhood, does it constitute probable cause? No. Am I profiling? No. Am I curious? You bet your life I am. Am I going to stop him? That depends. Look, what I'm saying is that a case simply cannot be made against officers as our uninformed African American ministers and politicians seem so determined to do. What? Absolutely not! We have no concrete data or sufficient factual evidence to support the argument that seventy percent of our searches are blacks and Latinos. As a matter of fact, I doubt whether any of you people have such evidence. Now, if you folk will excuse me, I have another urgent interview coming up. Good night and God bless.

Lights down on police commissioner. Music up and out.

Scene Five

Pennsylvania Interstate. Lights up on Big T and family. Josie reads, glancing quickly at the speedometer. Tyrone notices cop in rearview mirror.

TYRONE:	We've got company.
JOSIE:	I told you to stick to the speed limit.
TYRONE:	I am sticking to the speed limit.
JOSIE:	You were five miles over.
TYRONE:	Other people are ten miles over.
JOSIE:	Be quiet and pull over.
TYRONE:	I'm pulling over.
NAOMI:	What they stopping us for? T Baby, wake up.
BIG T:	What's going on?
NAOMI:	State trooper is pulling us over.
BIG T:	Let me get a look.
JOSIE:	Keep your hands in view at all times.
TYRONE:	My hands are in view.
JOSIE:	Be calm.
TYRONE:	You're making me nervous, okay?
BIG T:	He looks harmless from here.
NAOMI:	Look to me like he's from *CHiPs*.
BIG T:	Naomi, this ain't no TV show.
JOSIE:	Pull out your license and registration.
TYRONE:	Nobody asked for license and registration.
JOSIE:	You know it's the first thing they ask for.
TYRONE:	They have to tell you why they stopped you first.
JOSIE:	Tyrone Matthew Bankston Gerard . . .
TYRONE:	Why don't you say it, all right?
JOSIE:	Say what?

TYRONE:	You know what.
JOSIE:	I *don't* know what.
TYRONE:	Heather Marie Jordan!
NAOMI:	(*Excited.*) Heather is in the wedding too?
BIG T:	Calm down. Ain't nobody committed no crime. Best you folk keep your eyes on Smokey. Don't want him planting nothing on my Eldorado.
NAOMI:	I hear they're doing that to black folk in this part of the country.
BIG T:	They'll do it anywhere in these United States, Naomi.

The state trooper, wearing motorcycle helmet, steps up to car.

STATE TROOPER:	You folk know why I stopped you?
TYRONE:	No, sir, afraid not.
STATE TROOPER:	Checking to see if you're wearing your seat belts.
BIG T:	We've been buckled up since we left Chicago.
STATE TROOPER:	Chicago? (*Unable to mask his admiration at the Cadillac.*) Eldorado Biarritz. Talk about the good old days. Didn't know they made seat belts for this one.
BIG T:	They don't. My grandson here, Tyrone, he installed the seat belts.
STATE TROOPER:	Yeah? Where you folk headed?
BIG T:	Tyrone is a automotive design engineer at Michigan University. He modernized this Cadillac for his senior thesis.
STATE TROOPER:	Where did you say you folk headed?
TYRONE:	Virginia.
BIG T:	Spending the night in DC to see my son, Little T.
STATE TROOPER:	Little T works for Uncle Sam, does he?
BIG T:	He's enshrined on the Vietnam Memorial.
STATE TROOPER:	Sorry to hear that. This is your car?
BIG T:	I'm the owner.
STATE TROOPER:	You're the sole owner?
BIG T:	You're speaking to the sole owner.

State trooper looks closer at odometer—curious, suspicious.

STATE TROOPER:	I'm curious. How many times has your odometer turned over?
BIG T:	It ain't never turned over.
NAOMI:	It's been jacked up on four blocks.
BIG T:	He's talking to me, sweetheart. It's been jacked up on four blocks.
NAOMI:	Except for your spring tune-up.
BIG T:	Except for my spring tune-up.
STATE TROOPER:	How come it sat on the blocks so long?
BIG T:	Naomi?
NAOMI:	That is *not* his business.
BIG T:	You don't want to know that, mister.
STATE TROOPER:	You telling me or not?
NAOMI:	Didn't you hear him say you don't want to know?
STATE TROOPER:	You folk got something against telling me why this Cadillac sat on the blocks so long? (*They don't respond.*) Tyrone, how come this car sat on the blocks so long?
TYRONE:	Granddad, how come Molly sat on the blocks so long?
BIG T:	Naomi, what you want me to tell this here fellow about this Cadillac?
NAOMI:	T. Baby, let the *dead* bury the *dead*.
BIG T:	I ain't got a thing more to say about this Cadillac.
STATE TROOPER:	Tyrone?
TYRONE:	Yes, sir?
STATE TROOPER:	Where were you born?
TYRONE:	What?
JOSIE:	Chicago, Presbyterian.
STATE TROOPER:	Excuse me, ma'am, Tyrone is big enough to answer for himself.
JOSIE:	Officer? Do you remember where you were born?
STATE TROOPER:	I'm the one asking the questions, okay, ma'am?
TYRONE:	I was born in Chicago, Presbyterian.
JOSIE:	I am not done speaking, Tyrone. Officer, unless I am terribly mistaken, this is the Commonwealth of Pennsylvania, not the Mexican border.
STATE TROOPER:	You, young man, where were your grandparents born?

TYRONE:	What—Granddad . . .
BIG T:	Mississippi!
NAOMI:	Heaslip County, Mississippi!
BIG T:	I's born in Heaslip, Mississippi.
STATE TROOPER:	Mind if I see your license and the registration to this car?
BIG T:	No, sir, I don't mind at all.
STATE TROOPER:	I'm speaking to Tyrone.
NAOMI:	Tyrone doesn't mind at all.
TYRONE:	Not at all, Grandma. I have them right here.

Tyrone passes information to state trooper.

JOSIE:	Excuse me, officer. Is there a problem?
STATE TROOPER:	A problem, ma'am?
JOSIE:	Yes, a problem. I want to know if there is a problem.
STATE TROOPER:	Not that I can see.
JOSIE:	Then why in God's name are we sitting here on the Pennsylvania Turnpike like a bunch of bandits?
STATE TROOPER:	You folk have a nice day.
TYRONE:	(*Driving off.*) Thank you, sir.
NAOMI:	If that ain't the living gall!
BIG T:	Where was you born, boy? (*Amused.*) Uh . . . uh . . . ah . . .
JOSIE:	Why my child was born in the hospital, just like you, officer.
BIG T:	"Boy, where was your grandmammy and your grandpappy born?" Hell, when I heard that, I forgot myself where I was born. (*They crack up with laughter, all but Tyrone.*) Uh . . . uh . . . uh, I's born in ah . . . ah . . . ah, Miss-Mississi-Mississippi!
TYRONE:	It's not funny! He was trying to get a handle on my accent.
JOSIE:	You know what you are to that man?
TYRONE:	That man was profiling us.
JOSIE:	If that fellow was looking for the real drug dealers, he'd be shaking down white kids in suburban high schools and colleges.

BIG T:	He ain't allowed to make his search on the backs of folk who look like him.
NAOMI:	Amen to that.
BIG T:	Tell you now. I ain't consenting to nobody searching my Cadillac.
NAOMI:	Be careful what you say, T Baby. That man is on the phone calling us in this very second.
BIG T:	Nonsense, Naomi!
NAOMI:	Mark my word.
BIG T:	You getting paranoid.
NAOMI:	That man isn't done with us. Tyrone, I told you to cut that mess off your head. You're liable to be the reason we got stopped.
TYRONE:	What's my hair got to do with us being stopped?
NAOMI:	You are a Rastafarian drug dealer to that man.
TYRONE:	I don't smoke. I don't do cocaine. I don't booze, and I don't chase wild women.
NAOMI:	That's fine, but I want you to look like a gentleman for your sister's wedding.
TYRONE:	Grandma?
NAOMI:	What is it, baby?
TYRONE:	*You're profiling me!*
NAOMI:	You are going to ruin the sightline standing up there in a tuxedo looking like a Buckwheat ragdoll. You know how handsome you look with your haircut.
BIG T:	Naomi, why don't you flat out tell the boy to cut his hair for Denise's wedding?
NAOMI:	I can't do that, T Baby.
BIG T:	You tell me to cut mine whenever you damn well please.
NAOMI:	I don't want the child at the wedding with his mouth poked out and rolling his eyes at me. T Baby, please ask your grandson in the kindest manner possible to cut his hair for his sister's wedding?
BIG T:	I'm not telling Tyrone to cut his hair.
NAOMI:	Good heavens, T Baby! You're the child's granddaddy!
BIG T:	Tyrone can wear his dreadlocks all the way down to his black behind as far as I'm concerned.

NAOMI:	Shame on you! Josie, dear, do you mind asking your son to cut his hair?
JOSIE:	Mama, don't even go there.
NAOMI:	You're the child's mama. Is it too much for a mother to ask her son to cut his hair for his sister's wedding?
JOSIE:	I am the last person in the world to ask, "Tyrone, would you please cut your hair for your sister's wedding?"
NAOMI:	Tyrone, baby, if you don't mind my saying so, you are the most handsome young man on God's earth. I know all the bridesmaids will be swooning all over you.
TYRONE:	With or without my dreadlocks, Grandma?
NAOMI:	All those dreadlocks! You're going to steal the show from the bride! I know you are not that selfish.
TYRONE:	Okay, okay, I hear you, Grandma!
NAOMI:	Tyrone, baby . . .
TYRONE:	Yes, Grandma, I still love you.
NAOMI:	Praise the Lord! You're God's gift to your grandma.
BIG T:	Naomi, you think we did the right thing by taking this car off the blocks? I told you to accept Abe Tillman's offer.
NAOMI:	I am not hearing it, T Baby! Denise and Howard are riding from the church to the reception in Molly.
BIG T:	Forty thousand dollars, Naomi!
NAOMI:	Everything in life isn't about making money.
BIG T:	Go on. Suit yourself.
TYRONE:	Granddad, how come Molly sat on the blocks so long? Granddad . . .
JOSIE:	Keep your eyes on the road, Tyrone.
TYRONE:	My eyes are on the road. Granddad . . .
NAOMI:	Didn't you hear me say let the dead bury the dead?
TYRONE:	Granddad?
BIG T:	Boy, I know you heard your grandma.
TYRONE:	Go on! Take it to your grave. A whole lot of good that is going to do me. Is anybody listening?
NAOMI:	T Baby, are we taking it to our graves?
BIG T:	Let the *dead* bury the *dead*, Naomi.

JOSIE:	Amen.
TYRONE:	Granddad?
JOSIE:	Tyrone . . .
BIG T:	I'm listening.
TYRONE:	The dead has a way of coming back to haunt the living.

Lights fade as silence descends.

Scene Six

Police car. Spotlight rises on state trooper from earlier stop. He is calling in the Cadillac.

STATE TROOPER: I need you to run a check on a late-model Cadillac. Eldorado Biarritz. Red! Refurbished interior. See what's stolen, missing. One black male, yeah, dreadlocks, around twenty-four, another I take to be mid-seventies. We got two black females. One appears to be middle to late forties, the other early to mid-seventies. Young black male behind the wheel. Bit nervous, you know, anxious, I'd say. The old man is shifty-eyed on the mileage question. Put a trail on them. They're stopping over in DC on their way to Virginia.

Lights fade on officer. "Highway to Heaven" fades in.

Scene Seven

Morning. Police Commissioner at press conference. Lights rise on Police Commissioner as music fades to background.

POLICE COMMISSIONER: Absolutely not! God forbid! No such thing! You people must understand one thing. A black person is not a suspect the minute he sets foot outside his home. Nope. Skin color does not constitute reasonable cause. What? Absolutely not! Being black in a fancy car is not probable cause. Nope. Being black in a car with tinted windows doesn't constitute probable cause either. The truth of the matter is this. We are color-blind when it comes to stops and searches. We'll stop anyone if there is probable cause. Don't confuse effective police work with racial bigotry. Well, now if you've got a dozen earrings dangling from your ears, your nose, lips, tongue, eyebrows, belly button, a spear through your nose, and a phone that's pricier than mine, it would be very difficult to turn a blind eye regardless of your color. Excuse me? What? No. I don't subscribe to stereotypes. What—no, I'm not prejudiced. That word doesn't exist in our department.

Lights fade on police commissioner.

Scene Eight

Afternoon. Virginia, Interstate 95. "Highway to Heaven" fades into background. Lights rise on patrol car. Two officers, Strick and Rock, are sitting in car.

ROCK:	What the hell? You see that?
STRICK:	Custom-made Eldorado.
ROCK:	Is that in your face or what? Grandma, grandpa, mama, and junior bear!
STRICK:	It's a family affair.
ROCK:	This is the one I've been waiting for.
STRICK:	What?
ROCK:	We've got a major haul on our hands, partner.
STRICK:	Yeah, big enough to land you a cushy gig in administration.
ROCK:	No way in hell! The street is my home.
STRICK:	Yeah, you gotta get your hands dirty.

ROCK:	Where you think they're hiding it? Tire rims, doors, and seats—whadda you say we move in on them?
STRICK:	She's not speeding.
ROCK:	Colored folk not speeding in an Eldorado? That makes them suspects.
STRICK:	Maybe they're out for a joyride.
ROCK:	Right! They're out for a joyride all the way from the "Land of Lincoln." I'll bet my career on it. We'll ask to do a search.
STRICK:	And if mama bear says yes?
ROCK:	God, I hate breaking in rookies! She'll say no. That means junior bear has planted the goods so deep inside the ass of that Eldorado until we'll need a pack of bloodhounds and a demolition team to dig it out. We got a report on a stolen Eldorado?
STRICK:	Naw.
ROCK:	We do now. Okay? Run a check on them. See what you can dig up.
STRICK:	You're sick.
ROCK:	Smart. I'm smart.
STRICK:	Yeah, Rock, you've got extra sensory perception.
ROCK:	And you, Strick? You got shit for brains. Plate number George Victor Howard 8371. See what you got on them. Put a trailer on them. Bring in Magnum. That German shepherd has got the best nose in the country.

Lights fade on Rock and Strick, while rising on Big T and family. Josie is behind the wheel. She checks rearview mirror.

Scene Nine

Few minutes later. Big T and family on the highway.

JOSIE:	We've got company.
NAOMI:	Mercy!
JOSIE:	I'm not speeding.
TYRONE:	Don't look at me. I didn't say anything.

BIG T:	What they want this time?
NAOMI:	I told you that man called us in.
BIG T:	Stop your nonsense, Naomi.
JOSIE:	Smokey had better have a mighty good reason for pulling me over.
TYRONE:	You're driving while black. That's good enough for him.
JOSIE:	That's not good enough for Jessie Jackson and Al Sharpton, and it sure isn't good enough for Josie Bankston Gerard.
BIG T:	Jessie Jackson is just another nigger in a Cadillac to these fools.

Rock approaches car.

ROCK:	You folk know why I stopped you?
JOSIE:	You've got a report on a stolen Eldorado, right?
ROCK:	You should signal when you change lanes, miss.
JOSIE:	Officer, I do signal when I change lanes. Is there anything else?
ROCK:	I'm asking the questions. Where you folk headed?
JOSIE:	Richmond, Virginia.
BIG T:	Stopping over in DC.
ROCK:	Checking out Abe Lincoln, are ya?
BIG T:	The Vietnam Memorial. My son, Little T, is on the wall.
ROCK:	My condolences. Excuse me, mind if I check your license?
JOSIE:	Not at all. (*Passing license to Rock.*) I have it right here.
ROCK:	You're Josie?
JOSIE:	It's my picture you're looking at.
ROCK:	May I see your—
JOSIE:	Registration and insurance? (*Whipping them out with unerring finesse.*) I thought you'd want to see them.
BIG T:	The car is registered in my name.
JOSIE:	Is there anything else?
ROCK:	Mind if we have a look inside the trunk?

JOSIE:	Do you have a search warrant?
ROCK:	I don't need a search warrant.
JOSIE:	Which means you have probable cause.
ROCK:	You letting me have a look or not?
BIG T:	The only drugs we got on board is for diabetes and high blood pressure.
NAOMI:	They right here in my purse if you want to see them.
ROCK:	Okay if I have a look in the trunk, Uncle?
BIG T:	That's Tyrone Wesley Bankston to you, officer.
ROCK:	Mr. Bankston, mind if I take a look inside your trunk?
NAOMI:	T Baby, I don't want that man . . .
BIG T:	(*Getting out of car.*) Naomi, I'm gonna let this here fellow have a look so we can get back on the road, okay?
NAOMI:	That man isn't putting his hands on Denise's dress.
BIG T:	Sweetheart . . .
NAOMI:	I hand-stitched my granddaughter's wedding dress.
BIG T:	He's not touching the dress. Go on, mister, search the men's belongings, but you can't touch the women's things.
ROCK:	I'm searching everything in the car.
NAOMI:	(*Getting out of car.*) Oh, no, you aren't.
TYRONE:	Grandma!
NAOMI:	Get back in the car, T Baby.
TYRONE:	Let him have a look so we can get on the road.
NAOMI:	I smell Doug Winston on that man!
JOSIE:	(*Getting out of the car.*) Oh my god. Mama!
NAOMI:	T Baby . . .
BIG T:	Naomi, he's not going to harm the dress.
NAOMI:	Get back in the car, T Baby.
BIG T:	Let him have a look!
NAOMI:	Over my dead body! Everybody get back in the car right this minute!
BIG T:	Calm down, sweetheart!
JOSIE:	Mama, get in the car.

NAOMI:	Get that man away from my car! Get him out of here this minute!
BIG T:	Mister, you can't search our car.
ROCK:	I'm holding you here until you comply with my request.
JOSIE:	Fine by me, so long as you provide us with a lawyer from the NAACP. And while you're at it, show probable cause. Driving while black won't cut it.
STRICK:	Rock!
ROCK:	What?
STRICK:	They're clean. You folk have a pleasant vacation.
JOSIE:	Thank God somebody has some sense around here.
ROCK:	Hey . . . (*Shooting Strick a look to kill.*) What the hell do you think you're doing?
STRICK:	They checked out okay.

Lights fade on Rock and Strick heading off. The family consoles a shaken Naomi as they get back in car.

NAOMI:	T Baby . . .
BIG T:	It's okay, sweetheart. It's okay. He didn't touch anything.
JOSIE:	Denise is going to look beautiful in her dress. And Tyrone is going to look real handsome in his new haircut.
NAOMI:	You think so, Josie?
TYRONE:	I know so, Grandma, Denise is going to steal the show in your Galvano wedding gown.
NAOMI:	Praise the Lord.
JOSIE:	Stark white is going to look gorgeous on my grandbaby.
TYRONE:	Gorgeous, Grandma, Denise is going to look absolutely gorgeous.
NAOMI:	God bless all of you!
TYRONE:	Grandpa? Is Doug Winston dead and buried too?
BIG T:	Dead and buried, Tyrone, just like old man Jim Crow.
TYRONE:	I wouldn't say Jim Crow is dead and buried.

BIG T: I said dead and buried. He is gonna stay that way. Is that clear?

Big T places arm around Naomi.

TYRONE: Yeah, Granddad, if you say so.
BIG T: I said so.
TYRONE: Got ya.

Lights fade on Big T and family as "Highway to Heaven" fades in.

Scene Ten

Police car. Lights rise on Rock and Strick in police car. Music fades out.

STRICK: Cat got your tongue?
ROCK: Never pull rank on me again.
STRICK: Pull rank?
ROCK: Fricking wop!
STRICK: Rock . . .
ROCK: Twenty-two years on the road. You think I don't know my job?
STRICK: What are you talking about?
ROCK: Didn't you get it?
STRICK: Get what?
ROCK: Grandma and Grandpa deserve an academy award for that good cop, bad cop routine. That Rastafarian Bob Marley wannabe didn't utter a word.
STRICK: Grandpa is a retired steel mill worker. Grandma is a retired nurse. Mama is a teacher. Junior is clean.
ROCK: You're brain-dead.
STRICK: What—
ROCK: I can smell the coke all the way to Cancun and back. I'm performing surgery on that Cadillac.
STRICK: The kid just graduated Michigan University in automotive design.

ROCK:	Michigan U hosts the biggest pot party in the country. And you're telling me junior bear isn't making a haul? It's a family affair.
STRICK:	No food wrappers on the floor. No day-old beards. Junior's pants aren't hanging from his ass.
ROCK:	Jesus, partner, two years ago, you remember? I let that car full of spooks slide. The guys in Wabash County land the cocaine haul of the century.
STRICK:	Yeah, yeah, Rock, you missed the big one.
ROCK:	They were all American spooks dressed in Sunday-go-to-meeting rags.
STRICK:	Yesterday it was the wops and the Jews.
ROCK:	Cost me, Rock, the biggest promotion of my life!
STRICK:	Today, it's the wetbacks and spooks.
ROCK:	Not if I land this haul.
STRICK:	Tomorrow it'll be the Arabs and—
ROCK:	What the fuck did you say to me? Whose side are you on, missy? I gotta know whose side you're on! You're either a patriot for the cause, or your ass is sleeping with the enemy! I don't want a limp dick traitor in my army. This is war, man! War! Me, I'm trying to help the spooks clean the scum from their own neighborhood. I climb into my car every day. Rock, the warrior, crusading against the menace that's destroying colored America. What does that make me? A goddamn red neck! The biggest pig in these United States of America! Why? I'm searching the sons of bitches who are dealing poison to their own brothers and sisters. I'd be a hero if I were a nigger nailing niggers. Where is Rock's medal? I want my medal! Somebody gonna give me my fucking medal! Paint my neck red, my ass white, and my eyes blue. This is war! Did you forget Wayne Hanson? He tried to reason with a coke runner. He's lying six feet under. You don't reason with these bastards. You contain them! By any means necessary! And don't talk to me about racial profiling! Carl—whoever the hell he is—that New Jersey police guy is right. Blacks and Latinos

push the cocaine and the pot. That guy should get the Medal of Honor. What did he get? His walking papers! Why? Because the governor wants to be president! Everybody profiles. The FBI, CIA, and DEA—those sons of bitches invented profiling. This country was built on ethnic profiling. Indians, Spics, Mics, Spooks, Wops, Kikes, Japs, Chinks, Dagos! Racial profiling is as American as apple pie! You're goddamn right. Rock profiles! When my boss says I don't, he's lying up the wazoo. Lying is his job. Digging for the truth is mine.

STRICK:	Where's the coke, Rock?
ROCK:	*Nobody ever listens to me!*
STRICK:	Where is it, man? Where is the coke?
ROCK:	You dumb fuck—you read between the lines.
STRICK:	Where is the goddamn coke?
ROCK:	The last place on earth I'm supposed to look.
STRICK:	Rock!
ROCK:	"I hand-stitched the wedding dress!"
STRICK:	Jeez . . .
ROCK:	*I hand-stitched the wedding dress!* Don't you get it?
STRICK:	God help you, Rock. "I hand-stitched my *granddaughter's* wedding dress."

Lights down on Rock and Strick. "Highway to Heaven" fades in.

ACT TWO

Scene One

Interstate rest stop. Picnic area. "Highway to Heaven" fades in. Lights rise on Big T and family at a roadside rest stop picnic table. The food is now an afterthought. Naomi is in wedding heaven.

NAOMI:	Michael is going to faint with joy when he sees his beloved coming down the aisle in all her glory. I'm liable to faint myself.
JOSIE:	Mama, please.
NAOMI:	Well, I just might.
JOSIE:	A wedding doesn't make a marriage.
NAOMI:	I know that, Josie.
JOSIE:	It's a ridiculously expensive fantasy that costs tens of thousands of dollars.
NAOMI:	Every bride is entitled to her fantasy for one day in her life.
JOSIE:	After that, it's back to the kitchen.
NAOMI:	At least, it won't be some white woman's kitchen. Anybody know why the bride wears white?
TYRONE:	She wears white because she's a virgin!
NAOMI:	She wears white because she's starting life anew filled with joy and happiness. When Michael places the ring on the fourth finger of Denise's left hand, he will feel the beating of his beloved's heart. Would-be suitors will know Denise is spoken for. They'll have to cast their wandering eye on some

	other single woman. Tyrone, baby? Did I mention to you that Denise is wearing my updated tiara?
TYRONE:	You didn't mention it to me, Grandma.
NAOMI:	She is! It's going to bring Denise good fortune and longevity.
JOSIE:	Mama, please . . .
NAOMI:	It's true. My tiara represents something old and something new to link this family for a thousand years hence. Denise will never be without wealth as long as she lives. Never, ever!
JOSIE:	You can't be certain about that.
NAOMI:	Oh, yes, I can be certain.
JOSIE:	No, you can't.
NAOMI:	Don't dispute me, Josie!
JOSIE:	How on earth do you know Denise is never going to be without wealth?
NAOMI:	I have personally seen to it.
JOSIE:	And just how have you seen to it yourself?
NAOMI:	I sewed two gold coins in each wedding slipper. You ought to know by now wealth isn't about how much money you have in dollars and cents. It's about where your heart and your soul are. A millionaire without dignity is a man with his soul in a garbage heap. Tyrone, baby, do you realize in ancient times a man won his bride by capturing her?
BIG T:	That's how I won mine.
NAOMI:	Mind your business, T Baby.
BIG T:	Well, I did, sweetheart.
TYRONE:	Granddad, you *captured* Grandma?
BIG T:	The groom still captures his bride today.
TYRONE:	Yeah? What does he *capture* her with?
BIG T:	His heart!
NAOMI:	Amen to that.
BIG T:	I gather that's how you captured that gal that's got your nose wide open as a river. See, in the old days, the best man accompanied the groom to help capture the bride.
NAOMI:	That's right, Tyrone.

BIG T:	The groom took his best man along so he'd be at the groom's side to help him fight off enemy suitors.
TYRONE:	The groom doesn't do that today.
BIG T:	Yes, he does. You notice how the groom keeps his right hand free at the wedding?
NAOMI:	There is a very important reason for that.
TYRONE:	Yeah? What?
BIG T:	Tell him, Naomi.
NAOMI:	In case somebody tries to capture his bride, he and his best man can protect her.
JOSIE:	Please! Weddings are a ridiculously outdated ritual that causes people to spend billions and billions of dollars!
NAOMI:	I know it's a ritual, Josie.
BIG T:	It's a ritual blessed by God.
NAOMI:	Rituals are what separate us from animals.
BIG T:	Your mama and me sent you to college to learn that much.
NAOMI:	Tyrone, dear, you make sure Heather knows she can't wear stark white for your wedding.
JOSIE:	Mama, must you bring up what's her name?
TYRONE:	Heather! Her name is Heather.
JOSIE:	I don't want to hear it!
NAOMI:	Calm yourself, Josie.
TYRONE:	Grandma, why can't Heather wear white?
NAOMI:	I didn't say she can't wear white, baby, I said she can't wear stark white. I expect you to know that. You are a designer.
TYRONE:	I design automobiles, not wedding dresses.
NAOMI:	You work with color.
TYRONE:	Color for cars, Grandma, not wedding dresses.
NAOMI:	Hush up and listen to what I'm saying!
TYRONE:	I want to know why my honey can't wear stark white.
NAOMI:	Stark white washes out against pale skin. A blue-eyed blonde chooses off white for her dress. Come to think of it, a princess design would look absolutely divine on Heather's pageboy figure.
JOSIE:	Please stop throwing hints.

NAOMI: It most certainly will, Josie! Heather is going to be ready to grace the cover of *Bridal Magazine* when I'm done dressing her. As a matter of fact, Heather and Tyrone will both be on the cover! Now that is going to be something to behold. *I'm stitching Heather's dress!*

JOSIE: I beg your pardon?

BIG T: Naomi . . .

NAOMI: I most certainly am, T Baby.

BIG T: No more talk about wedding dresses!

NAOMI: I'm saving the child nine thousand dollars!

BIG T: All I want is to walk my granddaughter down the aisle and give her to Michael.

JOSIE: Excuse me. You are not *giving* my daughter to anybody.

BIG T: She asked me to!

JOSIE: Slavery is over and done with.

BIG T: I'm not selling your daughter on the auction block. I'm reciting the wedding vows. Who gives this woman to this man? I do!

JOSIE: I've changed the wedding vows.

BIG T: You can't change God's rules.

JOSIE: Who said anything about changing God's rules?

BIG T: The wedding vows say a woman is supposed to love, honor and obey her husband. And the man is supposed to protect and cherish his wife.

NAOMI: That's the scripture, Josie! Love, honor and obey. Protect and cherish.

BIG T: I don't care if you rewrite the wedding vows a million times. It's still *love, honor and obey!* I've been obeying your mama fifty something years. That's a hell of a lot longer than she's obeyed me.

NAOMI: Did you know Mama was fourteen years old when Daddy claimed her for himself?

TYRONE: Fourteen! That's illegal!

BIG T: It wasn't illegal in our day.

TYRONE: What if she didn't like him?

BIG T: Tough luck, she was stuck with that sucker for the rest of her life.

NAOMI:	Do you mind, T Baby? I'm trying to finish my story.
BIG T:	Don't mind me, sweetheart. Go on.
NAOMI:	Thank you, love! Tyrone . . .
TYRONE:	I'm listening, Grandma.
NAOMI:	Grandpa Joe called his five daughters ages thirteen through nineteen. He lined them up for Papa Boatwright to have his pick of the litter.
TYRONE:	His pick of the litter? They weren't kittens and puppies.
NAOMI:	Behave and listen. Papa Boatwright's eyes fell on Mama Gertrude. Grandpa Joe said, "Gertrude, pack your bags and go keep house for Papa Boatwright." Mama Gertrude packed her bags and went to live with Papa Boatwright. He told her he was going to make a woman out of her. She ran away from Papa Boatwright and came back home the first night. Said he was way too much man for her. She was bleeding and hurting all inside. Grandpa Joe sent her back to Papa Boatwright kicking and screaming. Grandma Tina held her hand all the way back home to Papa Boatwright. Grandma Tina promised her it wouldn't hurt so bad after the first baby came. She was right. Eleven more babies came, seven boys and four girls. Mama stayed with Papa Boatwright sixty-two years, before the Lord called him to be with the saints.
TYRONE:	Granddad, you lucked out with Grandma.
BIG T:	Luck ain't got a thing to do with a successful marriage. We've been working at this marriage since the day we said I do.
TYRONE:	And you finally got it right.
BIG T:	I ain't saying I got it right. Lord knows I been working at it day and night.
NAOMI:	You've got to work at a marriage.
BIG T:	Night and day. Come rain or shine.
NAOMI:	Come rain or shine, you got to work at it.
BIG T:	Work at it in season and out of season!

NAOMI:	(*Overlapping with Big T.*) In season and out of season. If you don't work at it every day, next thing you know—
BIG T:	(*Finishing Naomi's sentence, as long-term couples often do.*) It's falling to pieces.
NAOMI:	That's right, falling to pieces.
BIG T:	(*Overlapping with Naomi.*) Falling apart like an old house.
NAOMI:	Just like an old house.
BIG T:	Always some part of it in need of repair.
NAOMI:	(*Overlapping with Big T.*) In need of repair. Always some part . . .
BIG T:	Always! Ain't that the truth!
NAOMI:	Lord knows it is!
BIG T:	But if you spend plenty enough time on the maintenance part . . .
NAOMI:	Maintenance part . . . You'll keep your marriage like brand-new.
BIG T:	(*Overlapping.*) Like brand-new.
NAOMI:	Mercy! Brand-new!
BIG T AND NAOMI:	Amen, brand-new!
JOSIE:	(*Through tears.*) Stop it!
NAOMI AND BIG T:	Josie!
JOSIE:	Please stop all this damn nonsense about weddings and marriage!
TYRONE:	All right, all right. If you don't want Heather at the wedding, tell me to my face.
JOSIE:	Did I say I didn't want her at the wedding?
TYRONE:	You didn't invite her to be in the wedding party. Denise already told me.
JOSIE:	Family comes first.
TYRONE:	Heather *is* family.
JOSIE:	*Your* family, not mine.
TYRONE:	So it's going be like that?
JOSIE:	You will not speak to your mother in that tone!

TYRONE:	Mom, here is the deal. Heather is going to law school at Michigan U. And I'm staying on for graduate school.

Josie starts to walk away.

JOSIE:	I'm not listening.
TYRONE:	You never let me finish.
JOSIE:	You will not blackmail me into including her in the wedding.
TYRONE:	Kwatrina isn't in the family.
JOSIE:	She would have been in the family if you hadn't taken up with what's her name.
TYRONE:	I didn't take up with Heather. Bulls take up with heifers down on the farm. Heather and I met. We fell in love. We are going to share our lives together! Why won't you be happy for us?
JOSIE:	You and Kwatrina were a union made in heaven. I watch your prom video over and over. I watched it just last night! You and Kwatrina are so beautiful together. Don't you remember the way you were?
TYRONE:	The way we *were*! What about the way we are now, today?
JOSIE:	Tyrone, I beg you, please don't tear apart what God has already joined together in heaven.
TYRONE:	You're talking about the way you want it to be, not the way it was, is, or ever will be.
JOSIE:	Kwatrina is my daughter-in-law!
TYRONE:	Get real. Kwatrina is engaged to a Howard University guy.
JOSIE:	Because you took up with what's her name!
TYRONE:	Mom, Heather Marie Jordan. It's not going to kill you to say the name of your future daughter in law. Heather Marie Jordan (*Josie refuses to say Heather's name.*) God, Mom, you know why Kwatrina said yes to being in the wedding?
JOSIE:	She wanted to be close to you.
TYRONE:	She didn't want to hurt your feelings. Katrina dropped me. Heather Marie Jordan. Say it. Please?

	Heather Marie Jordan. (*Storming off at Josie's refusal to say Heather's name.*) I'm taking the train to Virginia!
BIG T:	Tyrone! Get back here!
JOSIE:	He can go to hell for all I care.
TYRONE:	Stop acting out your ridiculous high school prom fantasy.
JOSIE:	Get out of my sight!
BIG T:	Josie . . .
JOSIE:	I don't want to lose my child.
BIG T:	I wasn't giving you to some unknown man when I walked you down the aisle. I told you to wait, but you insisted on being married before Tyrone was born so he'd have a father. Did your husband beat you?
JOSIE:	No, he didn't beat me.
BIG T:	So what went wrong?
JOSIE:	One of us had to grow up and become a parent to Tyrone.
TYRONE:	I can't argue with that.
NAOMI:	T Baby, what color is Kwa-Kwa-Kwatrina?
BIG T:	You ever heard of a white gal named Kwatrina?
NAOMI:	Black comes in all colors, T Baby. Is she light skinned, dark skinned, brown, beige, high yellow?
BIG T:	Why you asking all that, sweetheart?
NAOMI:	I must know what color material to select for Kwatrina's wedding dress.
BIG T:	Didn't you hear Tyrone? A Howard University fellow already asked for Kwatrina's hand.
NAOMI:	Then I'm stitching Heather's dress! I'm saving the child nine thousand dollars!
BIG T:	We'll never get to Virginia! Tyrone, get over here!
TYRONE:	Mom, Heather is flying into Dulles at midnight. Can we meet her at the airport together?
JOSIE:	I'll have to check my calendar.
TYRONE:	I'll be home for Thanksgiving only if Heather is invited.
BIG T:	You two gonna have to work this out another time. Let's hit the road.

NAOMI:	Tyrone has to find a barber.
BIG T:	Not now, Naomi! Little T ain't seen Molly off the blocks yet.
NAOMI:	Lord knows that's the truth.
JOSIE:	My brother can't see me like this. I have to change somewhere.
BIG T:	You looking just fine the way you are.
NAOMI:	T Baby . . . (*Taking Big T's arm.*) I don't know if I can see my son now.
BIG T:	It's all right, sweetheart.
NAOMI:	Josie.

Josie steps forward and takes Naomi's arm.

JOSIE:	It seems like he was here just yesterday.
BIG T:	Little T is always here. Lord knows he's dying to see Molly.
TYRONE:	Does Little T know why Molly stayed on the blocks so long? (*Noticing everyone is ignoring him.*) Yeah? No? Maybe?
BIG T:	Mind your own business, son.

Lights dim on Big T and family.

Scene Two

Washington, DC. Vietnam Memorial. "Precious Memories" fades in. Pictures of Little T with family in army uniform, all smiles. A final picture of Little T in uniform wearing a smile frozen in time is seen.

Verse
Precious Father, loving Mother
Fly across the lonely years
And old home scenes of my childhood
In fond memory appear

Chorus
Precious memories, how they linger
How they ever flood my soul
In the stillness of the midnight
Precious sacred scenes unfold

Music fades to background. Lights rise on Big T and family facing Vietnam Memorial. Naomi wipes away tears. Big T comforts her. Josie kneels. Tyrone looks on, curious, perplexed.

BIG T: Molly is as beautiful as she was the day I drove her off the dealership lot. Matter of fact, she looks a whole lot better if you ask me. Your nephew, Tyrone, Josie's boy, he outfitted Molly with color TV, seat belts, airbags, and modern air conditioning. I know you're proud of her. We on the way to Denise's wedding over in Richmond. She's riding from the wedding to the reception in Molly. Wish you was in the wedding party. (*Reassuring.*) It's okay. Knowing you, Little T, I know you having yourself one hell of a good time with your Vietnam buddies. (*Naomi whispers in Big T's ear.*) Naomi, your mama, hand-stitched Denise's wedding dress all by herself. (*Breaking down.*) Damn near drove me to the crazy house. Sure did. Mama saved Denise a whole heap of money. God is good, Little T. God is good.

JOSIE: Little T should be on this trip with us. I want him here with me.

BIG T: He is here, always will be.

JOSIE: My brother is dead. Turned to dust just like all the others. I miss him so much.

BIG T: (*Comforting Josie.*) Look at Tyrone. Little T is written all over him.

NAOMI: Lord knows he is.

JOSIE: I want a few minutes alone with my brother. Please.

Big T and Naomi move away, hand in hand. Tyrone walks a few feet and stops to observe Josie. "Precious Memories" fades in quietly. Josie tries to recite from God's Trombones.

JOSIE: And Moses . . . And Moses lifted his rod . . . (*Breaking into tears.*) I'm sorry, Little T. I came all prepared to recite it for you, but I haven't been able to finish it since you've been gone. (*Pulling letters from bag.*) I kept your promise, Little T. I kept your promise. Tyrone, take these.

Tyrone moves forward.

TYRONE: What promise?

Josie passes letters to Tyrone.

JOSIE: Mama and Daddy must never know how their son died. Everything is in here. Little T, I'm passing your letters on to Tyrone so he'll know the truth.

TYRONE: How did Uncle T die?

JOSIE: He started protesting the war, he and a few buddies, while they were on tour in Vietnam. They punished him.

TYRONE: How so?

JOSIE: They made him walk point. Turned my brother into a human shield . . . silenced him with death . . . The details are in the letters. All Mama and Daddy know is that Little T was killed by the enemy and that he died a valiant death fighting for freedom and democracy. It's all they must ever know.

TYRONE: Does Uncle T know why Molly stayed on the blocks so long? (*Josie doesn't answer. Tyrone turns to Little T.*) I got a question for you.

JOSIE: Tyrone . . .

TYRONE: Uncle T. You want to tell me why Molly stayed on the blocks?

JOSIE: It's time for us to go.

TYRONE: I want to know.

JOSIE:	This isn't the place.
TYRONE:	If not here, then where?
JOSIE:	Just not here.

Tyrone escorts Josie away, glancing back at Little T.

Scene Three

Sunday. Church service. Fade into a rollicking version of James Cleveland's "Get Right Church and Let's Go Home." Lights rise on Big T and family in a United Methodist church. The atmosphere is as high spirited as any evangelical service. It is the climax of the early morning service. The fiery utterances of the minister punctuate the music. Josie is on her feet, in her glory. A voluptuous, sensuous quality permeates her movements. Naomi joins in, and before long, Big T and Tyrone are pulled into the fervor with song and dance. Josie goes into a toe-stumping holy dance with abandon. Tyrone and Big T clap until all four are caught up in the dance and music. They become one as they lose their inhibitions in the fervor of the moment. Big T glances at his watch. He gets Tyrone's attention, and they get Josie and Naomi.

| BIG T: | Time to hit the road, Josie. |

They depart the service, clinging to the beat of the music as they get into the car. Tyrone gets behind the wheel. Josie gets into the front seat on passenger side. Music fades to background.

BIG T:	Great day in the morning! Those Methodists got more fire in two pews than Crenshaw Baptist got in the whole church.
NAOMI:	Hallelujah! The blood is coursing through my veins like brand-new.
BIG T:	Mine too! Lord knows I'm heading to Christ United Methodist soon as we get back to Chicago.
NAOMI:	I didn't say we're changing memberships, T Baby.
BIG T:	It takes Sister Ester half the morning to read the announcements.
NAOMI:	That's how Sister Ester learned to read.
BIG T:	They printed right there in the bulletin.

NAOMI:	People like to hear them read aloud.
BIG T:	You mean some people like to hear them read aloud. I'm not one of them people. Josie, how did you know the minister was gonna speak on the children of Israel crossing the Red Sea?
JOSIE:	It was a coincidence.
NAOMI:	It's a sign God is with us.
BIG T:	Josie, do you recall my favorite sermon from *God's Trombones?* Just a couple of verses from "Let My People Go" is all I'm asking. (*Josie shakes her head.*) You had every sermon in *God's Trombones* memorized word for word on that trip to Mississippi. Never saw a person put a whole book between their ears like you. I'll bet my last dollar you recited it for Little T. (*Noticing Josie about to break into tears.*) It's okay if you ain't in the spirit now.
JOSIE:	Mama . . .
NAOMI:	Yes, dear?
JOSIE:	I just know Little T was thrilled to hear that you hand-stitched Denise's wedding dress. He's so proud of Mama. "Josie, you be sure to tell Mama Denise's dress puts Galvano to shame."
NAOMI:	Praise the Lord. I can't wait until Denise hears the news.
BIG T:	I hope you told Little T yours truly is escorting my granddaughter down the aisle?
JOSIE:	Yes, I broke the news.
BIG T:	Yeah, but did you tell him that I'm not allowed to *give* her away? What am I doing? *Presenting* her to the man in her life? (*Placing arm around Naomi.*) Thank God Papa Boatwright gave me his lovely daughter. If he hadn't, guess who wouldn't be around to prevent me from giving her granddaughter away?
NAOMI:	Behave, T Baby.
TYRONE:	Granddad.
BIG T:	Yeah, what is it, son?

| TYRONE: | How come Molly sat on the blocks so long? (*Silence descends.*) Granddad . . . Grandma . . . What's this? The cat's got everybody's tongue? |

"Highway to Heaven" fades in. Lights down on Big T and family.

Scene Four

Sunday. Later. Lights rise on Rock and Strick in unmarked car. Music fades.

ROCK:	I'll be a son of a bitch. Look at that, partner. That Eldorado is back! Hold on . . . They've got a new driver. Naw! It's junior bear. I'll be damned if the kid didn't cut his dreads! SOB. He's trying to pull a fast one on Rock. Check him out. He's cruising at seventy. Gonna let junior bear make it to seventy-five. Come on, kid. You gotta go seventy-five. Only way you can keep up with the traffic on Interstate 95. Come on, junior bear. He's picking up speed. Two more miles! Seventy-three, seventy-four . . . God, I don't believe it! Way to go, junior bear! Hallelujah! Call for backup. I'm performing an autopsy on that Eldorado.
STRICK:	He's slowing down.
ROCK:	He knows we're on to him. Naw, he doesn't, not in an unmarked car!
STRICK:	Rock, we got probable cause?

Rock eyes Strick with a mixture of contempt and suspicion.

ROCK:	Yeah, we got probable cause. I got probable cause.
STRICK:	Rock . . .
ROCK:	You got probable cause, okay?
STRICK:	I do?
ROCK:	You do.
STRICK:	Rock . . .
ROCK:	We'll chill out in the background. Give them plenty of time to arrange the next deal.

STRICK:	It's Sunday, Rock
ROCK:	And Jesus is in his holy temple.

Lights fade out on Rock. "Highway to Heaven" fades in.

Scene Five

Sunday. Later. Big T and family on the highway. Lights rise on Big T and family. Tyrone listens to rap music through headphones. Josie glances at meter.

BIG T:	Baby (*Cuddling up with Naomi.*), I wish we had that convertible. We could let the top down and feel the breeze flow through our lovely hair. Look at Queen Naomi. Don't tell me you made this outfit.
NAOMI:	I made it while I stitched Denise's wedding dress.
BIG T:	You look pretty as the day you did when we started going together in tenth grade. You know that?
NAOMI:	You started making eyes at me in eighth grade.
BIG T:	And who kissed me in fourth grade?
NAOMI:	(*Shrieking in embarrassment.*) Aaaaaaa! T. Baby . . .
BIG T:	Oh, yes, you did.
NAOMI:	I can't believe you said that.
BIG T:	Church Bible school.
NAOMI:	Shame on you!
BIG T:	Don't play like you forgot.
NAOMI:	You know puppy love doesn't count.
BIG T:	Counted for me. That kiss stayed on my cheek a whole week. Then Mama says to me, "Boy, wash your dusty face!" I go, "Okay, but I ain't washing off sweet Naomi's kiss."
NAOMI:	Oh, stop it.
BIG T:	I can still see you floating down that aisle on Papa Boatwright's arm, coming to meet me.
NAOMI:	T Baby . . .
BIG T:	I didn't see some stained woman covered in red. I saw the most beautiful rose to ever come out of the Mississippi Delta walking down that aisle. Do you know that, Naomi?

NAOMI:	God hears you, T Baby.
BIG T:	He'd better hear me. I can still taste your wedding kiss. Woman, you left enough sweetness inside me to last until Gabriel sounds his trumpet. Roses, Naomi, they are the only thing I ever smelled on you all these years. Beautiful red roses!
NAOMI:	How come you waited fifty years to tell me?
BIG T:	Oh, you mean to tell me you didn't already know?
NAOMI:	I knew, T Baby. I already knew.
BIG T:	My Delta Rose! Petals from heaven fall on me.
NAOMI:	Oh, stop it!
BIG T:	I'm in the mood to watch a little TV. Like *The Bold and the Beautiful.* How about you?
NAOMI:	It's Sunday, T Baby. Lawd today! Look at Tyrone. He's cute as a bug's behind in his new hairdo. There isn't a mother I know who wouldn't want her daughter to bring my grandbaby home for dinner. Tyrone?
TYRONE:	Yes, Grandma?
NAOMI:	I'm so proud of you.
BIG T:	He looks a lot like me the day we got hitched.
TYRONE:	I have a question for you.
JOSIE:	Keep your eyes on the road, Tyrone.
TYRONE:	My eyes are on the road. Granddad . . .
BIG T:	Eyes on the road, Tyrone.
TYRONE:	It's not about why you kept Molly on the blocks.
BIG T:	Good. Nothing else you ask me is off-limits.
TYRONE:	What makes a good marriage last?
BIG T:	Everything I said before and some. Until death do us part!
TYRONE:	You're telling me you've never ever been unfaithful?
BIG T:	Never ever.
NAOMI:	Amen!
TYRONE:	Never ever, Granddad?
BIG T:	Never ever—not in my heart.
NAOMI:	Excuse me? You'd better explain that "never ever in my heart" business.
TYRONE:	We can drop the subject if you want.

NAOMI:	Over my dead body. (*Noticing Big T hesitate.*) Commence to talking, T Baby.
BIG T:	Oh, well now, like, uh, uh . . .
NAOMI:	Don't you stutter on me.
JOSIE:	Speak the speech, I pray you, trippingly on the tongue.
TYRONE:	Suit the action to the word, the word to the action.
NAOMI:	Cut the Shakespeare. I'm waiting, T Baby.
BIG T:	(*With measured speech.*) It wasn't long after we joined Crenshaw Baptist when this particular church member—
JOSIE:	A holy roller! Hallelujah!
NAOMI:	I have a few other names for that heifer, but being that we just set foot outside church—
BIG T:	I can't go on with my story so long as you all keep on interrupting me. (*Everybody stops in anticipation.*) Any way, ah . . . ah . . . (*Halting, cautiously.*)
NAOMI:	I'm *listening*, T Baby.
BIG T:	You see, it was this particular Sunday, when Mrs. Whatchamacallher—
TYRONE:	Mrs.!
JOSIE:	I know he did not say *Mrs.*
NAOMI:	Stop the car, Tyrone!
TYRONE:	We're running late, Grandma.
NAOMI:	Stop the car, or I'm stopping your behind dead in your tracks.
JOSIE:	(*Noticing Big T is sweating.*) Tyrone, pass your granddaddy a hand full of tissues to wipe his brow.
NAOMI:	To whom was Mrs. Whatchatmacallher married?
BIG T:	You don't want to know that.
NAOMI:	I'm not asking you again.
BIG T:	The preacher.
NAOMI:	Leola Shackleford!
BIG T:	She was making her rounds with the entire deacon board.
TYRONE:	Granddad, the preacher's wife?

BIG T:	You folk gonna let me finish or not? (*They quiet down.*) Pastor Shackleford, he went on ahead to visit one of the sick members. Leola promised him she'd get a ride home. She made a beeline for my car.
NAOMI:	I know what kind of *ride* Leola was after.
BIG T:	No sooner than Pastor Shackleford was out the door, Leola jumps in my car. I ain't even out of sight of the church before she grabs my hand and places it on her . . . furry kitten.
TYRONE:	Pass some tissues my way.
JOSIE:	It's getting hot in Virginia.
BIG T:	I *removed* my hand and placed it back on the steering wheel. I did! Leola, she burst into tears! You all gotta understand something here. The hardest thing in the world for a red-blooded man to do is turn down a woman in need.
NAOMI:	You mean a *bitch in heat!*
TYRONE:	*Grandma!* Would you like some tissues?
NAOMI:	I'm cool as a cucumber, thank you. Go on.
BIG T:	Well, anyway, what's her name . . .
JOSIE, TYRONE, AND NAOMI:	*Leola!*
BIG T:	She says Pastor Shackleford howls like a German shepherd in the pulpit, but he is a Chihuahua in bed. She grabs my hand and puts it right back on her . . . ah . . . you know . . .
JOSIE, TYRONE, AND NAOMI:	*Furry kitten!*
BIG T:	"Leola! I'm a happily married man. I promised the Lord God above I'd never misbehave with the preacher's wife." The poor woman broke down in tears.
NAOMI:	How long did your hand rest on the preacher's wife's *furry kitten*?
BIG T:	I didn't have a stopwatch, Naomi.
NAOMI:	Big T, you can time a minute better than a million-dollar Rolex.

TYRONE:	They say if your hand stays on more than three seconds—
BIG T:	Boy, shut you damn mouth!
NAOMI:	Did this encounter with the preacher's wife occur in my Cadillac?
BIG T:	No way. She was in my doo doo brown Impala.
NAOMI:	Drive on, Tyrone.
TYRONE:	Grandma? Have you ever been unfaithful to your beloved husband all these years?
BIG T:	Boy, how dare you disrespect Grandma!
TYRONE:	No disrespect intended. But how am I to know if I don't ask?
BIG T:	Naw! My honey has never ever been unfaithful. (*After an uneasy moment, noticing Naomi isn't nodding in agreement.*) Sweetheart, have you ever, you know, been . . .
NAOMI:	(*Triumphant.*) Never ever! Not in my heart.
BIG T:	Hit the brakes on this damn Eldorado.
TYRONE:	We're three hours late!
BIG T:	Boy, don't make me jack *your* ass up on four blocks. (*Turning to Naomi.*) You want to explain that "not in my heart business"?
NAOMI:	For all you know, while you were out playing *doctor* with the preacher's wife, the preacher was checking my temperature. You do know what everyone says about Chihuahuas. Umm! They're cheerful, loving, attentive, and so sensitive to the touch. (*Placing her arms around Big T's shoulder and snuggling to heighten the tease. She rubs it in with a few seductively cute barks.*) They have a special thing for lying next to you and nudging you in *all the right places.*
BIG T:	(*Pulling away.*) That yelping Chihuahua ain't got nothing on my German shepherd.
NAOMI:	T Baby, dear, there is one thing you ought to have learned after fifty years of marriage. (*As Big T stares with a question mark spread across his face.*) It's not the size of the ship. It's the motion on the ocean.
TYRONE:	Ouch! (*Driving on.*) I'm back on the road.

BIG T:	I want to know one thing. Did you or did you not open my door for that damn Chihuahua?
NAOMI:	How long did it take you to get your hands off of Leola's furry kitten?
BIG T:	I damn near broke my wrist getting my hand back on the steering wheel. You know why, don't ya? My honey has all the right moves. (*Embracing Naomi.*) You know what the Bible says about love. "Love keeps no record of wrongs. Love always protects, always trusts." Come on, help your honey out.
NAOMI AND BIG T:	"Love endures all things. Love never fails." Amen!
TYRONE:	(*Noticing approaching car.*) Guess what, folk? We've got company.
JOSIE:	You were speeding off like a bat out of hell.
TYRONE:	I had to blend in with the traffic.
JOSIE:	Pull over, Tyrone.
TYRONE:	I'm pulling over.
NAOMI:	That's the same man who stopped us before. T Baby, something isn't right.
BIG T:	Everything is okay, Naomi.
NAOMI:	Not the way those men are moving.

The two officers charge up to the car.

ROCK:	This look like the Indy 500 to you, son?
JOSIE:	He was doing seventy.
ROCK:	Speed limit is sixty-five. Step out the car.

Tyrone gets out of car.

STRICK:	Hands in the air.

Rock shoves Tyrone against the car and searches him.

STRICK:	Everybody out the car.
JOSIE:	May I know what's going on?

Rock flashes search warrant.

ROCK:	You needed a search warrant? (*Flashing search warrant.*) You got it. Open the trunk.
BIG T:	What you searching for this time, mister?
NAOMI:	I don't want my things tampered with.
ROCK:	Quiet the old lady.
NAOMI:	T Baby, don't just stand there.
BIG T:	Ain't nothing I can do if they got authority to search.

Rock pulls out bag containing wedding dress.

NAOMI:	Don't you put your filthy hands on Denise's wedding dress!
ROCK:	One more word out of you, ma'am . . .
NAOMI:	I mean it, mister.
STRICK:	Hold on, partner. Ma'am, open your dress bag.
NAOMI:	I most certainly will not.
STRICK:	Mr. Bankston, open your wife's bag.
NAOMI:	You're not touching Denise's wedding dress.
STRICK:	Gotta see it, ma'am.
NAOMI:	This dress is *handmade*.
JOSIE:	Every stitch in it.
ROCK:	Hand-stitched wedding dress. You get it, partner?
TYRONE:	Get what? (*Realizing what is going on.*) You're not suggesting . . .
NAOMI:	T Baby . . .
BIG T:	Sweetheart, I'm gonna show these fellows we got nothing to hide from them.
NAOMI:	I'm having none of it.
BIG T:	Naomi . . .
TYRONE:	Open the bag so we can get on the road. Everybody driving by is staring at us.
ROCK:	*Somebody open the goddamn bag!*
TYRONE:	I'm opening it.
BIG T:	Wait. I'll do it.
NAOMI:	No, you're not. Let them do the devil's work.
JOSIE:	Mama, please.
NAOMI:	Quiet, Josie! If you men believe we're peddling drugs after just departing God's house of worship

on a Sunday morning, then you open that bag. Go on. Defile Denise's wedding dress with your filth and lust.

STRICK: (*Pulling Rock aside.*) I'm not messing with them.

ROCK: What the hell is this voodoo bullshit? You jinxed or what?

STRICK: I'm out of here.

ROCK: The hell you are. The car stopped twice in the last fifteen minutes. Get your ass over there and tell them you believe colored folk in a customized Eldorado Biarritz with Illinois plates, cruising Interstate 95 would never be caught harboring drugs. Then tell them they are free to go because we are a couple of clowns who just made assholes out of ourselves. Hey, partner, those drugs turn up when I rip open that bag and your chicken ass isn't backing me up.

STRICK: Fuck you, Rock. I'm out, man!

ROCK: Don't walk away from me, punk.

STRICK: You stopping me, Rock? Huh? (*In Rock's face.*) You're kicking my ass?

ROCK: Yesterday, that kid had dreadlocks halfway to Jamaica. Today, he's wearing a Joe College crew cut. You figured that one out, Einstein?

STRICK: My brother wears blond dreadlocks down to his ass. If that ain't enough for you, he's an education major with a concentration in Africana studies. I got one more for ya, Rock. Right now, he's on the road. Biking—from Ghana to Timbuktu!

ROCK: Yeah, he's gonna marry an African woman. And you're banging a couple of black chicks on the side.

STRICK: Fucking bite me.

ROCK: (*Snatching Strick back as he starts to walk away.*) Bitch! Don't walk away from me. I know about Wayne Hanson and you. You stopped that car two hours earlier. And you let them folk go free. And when you let them go, it's like you pulled the trigger that killed Wayne. You, man, you gonna snuff out your partner? Hey? Listen to me. Magnum is sniffing out the coke. When she scores, I'm wiping my ass with your uniform and serving you up as regurgitated dog food. Move your lame ass out this second, and don't you screw it up for me.

STRICK: Hey, folk. (*Moving forward.*) We've got a job to do. Best you people not obstruct us.

BIG T: Naomi, I'm opening the bag.

NAOMI: T Baby . . .

BIG T: Let them have a look. Okay, baby? (*Naomi stares anxiously as Big T unzips bag.*) See, here.

ROCK: Take it out of the bag. I gotta see for myself.

NAOMI: T Baby . . .

BIG T: Josie, give me a hand with the bag. (*Josie and Big T pull bag from trunk.*) My honey hand-stitched a thousand beads to this dress.

TYRONE: Fifty dollars a yard Grandma paid for the materials.

JOSIE: Every stitch in it is from my mother's heart.

ROCK: I gotta have a closer look. Unzip the bag.

NAOMI: T Baby . . .

BIG T: Naomi, I've got it, sweetheart.

Big T unzips bag and pulls dress out with Josie's help.

ROCK: Hand-stitched, hey?

NAOMI: Hand-stitched . . .

ROCK: (*Propelled forward by an irresistible urge to search dress.*) I gotta see it for myself.

Rock grabs dress and runs his hand down it as if searching someone for criminal evidence.

NAOMI: (*Shocked, horrified.*) Don't you—

JOSIE: (*Slapping Rock's hand away, unintentionally elbowing him to protect dress.*) Naaaaw!

BIG T: (*Leaping forward with Tyrone to restrain Josie.*) Josie!

TYRONE: Mama!

NAOMI: Oh god.

Rock stands in shock.

ROCK:	Don't just stand there, partner! Where the hell is backup?
STRICK:	Ma'am, you assaulted a police officer.
JOSIE:	Didn't you see what he did to Mama's dress?
STRICK:	(*Moving Josie away, pulling out handcuffs.*) Gotta take you in, ma'am . . .
TYRONE:	(*Protesting to Strick.*) Where are you taking my mother?
BIG T:	(*Grabbing Tyrone.*) Tyrone! Stay put.
STRICK:	(*Taking Josie away.*) You have the right to remain silent.
JOSIE:	(*As she is led offstage with officer.*) Mama . . .
NAOMI:	(*Staring at dress.*) T Baby, he's ruined Denise's wedding dress.
BIG T:	The dress is fine, Naomi.
NAOMI:	No, no, T Baby.
BIG T:	You see? (*Offering Naomi dress.*), There ain't a speck of dirt on it.
NAOMI:	Get that heap of trash away from me.

Big T and Tyrone carefully secure dress in bag.

BIG T:	Sweetheart, Denise loves her dress. We'll clean it. Make it brand-new. (*Naomi starts to walk to the police car with dress bag.*) Naomi, not Denise's dress!
NAOMI:	Can't you smell on that dress?

Naomi takes bag and places it on top of police car trunk. She speaks to Strick.

BIG T:	Naomi . . .
NAOMI:	You must know a nice young lady in need of a wedding gown. I'm saving the child nine thousand dollars. (*Looking around for Josie.*) Josie? Where is my daughter?

Naomi rushes out after Josie. Rock approaches Cadillac with ratchet. The first session of John Coltrane's "Alabama" fades in.

TYRONE:	What are you doing to Granddaddy's car?
ROCK:	Performing an autopsy.
TYRONE:	Granddad!
BIG T:	Tyrone . . .
TYRONE:	Hey, you—
ROCK:	Stand clear, kid!

Big T grabs Tyrone.

BIG T:	It's a car, son, not your life.

Rock pops off hubcaps as lights fade on a speechless Big T and Tyrone. "Alabama" rises, louder and louder.

Scene Six

Jail. Black police officer, Betty, enters following Josie into stark room. She wears rubber gloves and carries flashlight. "Alabama" fades out.

BETTY:	Disrobe, ma'am.
JOSIE:	What?
BETTY:	Disrobe, ma'am.
JOSIE:	No, I won't.
BETTY:	Disrobe completely.
JOSIE:	I can't.
BETTY:	Disrobe completely.
JOSIE:	Where's Mama?
BETTY:	The next room. Disrobe, ma'am.

Josie removes her shoes and then her stockings. She removes her dress, slip, and then hesitates.

BETTY:	You are to disrobe completely, ma'am. (*As Josie hesitates.*) Completely, disrobe completely.
JOSIE:	My panties too?
BETTY:	Completely, ma'am.

Josie removes her panties. A mixture of pain and shock spreads across her face.

BETTY:	(*With flashlight, probing.*) Open your mouth. Your ears, ma'am. Widen your nostrils. Raise your armpits. Higher, ma'am. Raise your breasts.
JOSIE:	What?
BETTY:	Your breasts. Raise your breasts.
JOSIE:	I have nothing under my breast.
BETTY:	Your breast, ma'am, raise your breast!
JOSIE:	I told you—
BETTY:	Your breast! Okay, ma'am, walk to the wall, turn and face me. Turn around and face me. Bend over. Bend over, ma'am. Bend over! Spread your cheeks. Spread your cheeks. Squat. Squat, ma'am. Cough. Cough, ma'am.

Josie coughs. The officer moves up behind Josie.

JOSIE:	(*Josie turns and shouts in defiance.*) Don't you touch me!

The startled officer quickly composes herself.

BETTY:	Get dressed, ma'am.
JOSIE:	Where's Mama?
BETTY:	Get dressed, ma'am.
JOSIE:	Mama—
BETTY:	Get dressed, ma'am.

"Alabama" fades in. Betty departs. Josie puts her clothes on.

JOSIE:	Mama, Mama . . . Oh god. (*Fearfully.*) Where is she? (*Suddenly screaming.*) Mama!

"Alabama" builds into next session.

Scene Seven

Thruway. Lights rise on Big T, Tyrone, Rock, and Strick on side of highway. The Cadillac has been dismantled. The doors are on the ground and the hubcaps and tires thrown aside. Big T is beyond anger. "Alabama" fades out.

ROCK:	(*Broken.*) Grandpa. You gonna tell me where the coke is? I won't arrest you. (*Solicitous.*) Grandpa . . .
BIG T:	I already told you. You've got the wrong folk.
STRICK:	You gentlemen look clean to me. (*Passing ratchet to Tyrone.*) You're gonna need this.
BIG T:	You ain't putting my car back together?
STRICK:	That's not my job.
BIG T:	What is your *job*, mister?
STRICK:	Next time you're pulled over by an officer of the law, stay calm and do as you're told. Tow truck is on the way.
TYRONE:	My grandfather's car isn't junkyard trash!
BIG T:	Tyrone . . .
STRICK:	Rock, we gotta go.
ROCK:	Grandpa, tell me where it is.
STRICK:	Rock . . .
ROCK:	Not until Grandpa tells me where it is. Tell me where you hid the goddamn coke!
BIG T:	In your head, mister. The drugs buried so deep in your mind until there ain't a German shepherd in the world can sniff them out. Best you get to digging. I'm gonna pray for you. I'm praying with all my might, because if I don't pray, I'm going looking for Doug Winston. God knows you don't want me to do that.
STRICK:	You'll wake up tomorrow and come looking for this. (*Handing Big T Naomi's wedding dress.*) I know it's trash to you now, but it'll be priceless this time tomorrow.
ROCK:	Grandpa . . .
STRICK:	On your feet, Rock.

Strick pulls Rock up. They head out.

TYRONE:	Granddad.
BIG T:	Never should have allowed this piece of crap off the blocks.
TYRONE:	Don't say that. I'm putting Molly back together.
BIG T:	This damn Cadillac brings out the evil in people.
TYRONE:	Granddad, do you know how many times I've been stopped and searched? Walking the street with my buddies? Going to a movie with Heather? Parked behind the steering wheel wolfing down a burger? Here's the clincher. I'm a passenger in a taxi. One of New York's finest pulls the taxi over, snatches me out, shoves me up against the car, and then pushes his hand into my chest to make sure I'm shaking like I'm scared to death. He's beating me bloody, and all the time I'm pleading for this black female officer in his car to intervene. She turns away in shame. Then he says, "Sorry, kid, mistaken identity. The taxi fare is on me. Have a nice day!" (*Noticing Big T chuckling.*) It's not funny. (*Big T laughs harder, a bitter edge to his laughter.*) Stop laughing! It's humiliating and you're laughing like a damn hyena!
BIG T:	I know you ain't telling Granddaddy to stop laughing.
TYRONE:	Guess what happened to me on the way to pick you up for the trip? Caught! Driving while black! Ha ha ha!
BIG T:	Boy, take a good look at the headlights on that Cadillac. What do you see? You can't see anything standing way over there. Come closer, closer, son. (*Tyrone squats.*) What do you see?
TYRONE:	Dirt, grime, grit, bugs.
BIG T:	You see any gnat shit?
TYRONE:	(*Taken aback.*) Any what?
BIG T:	Gnat shit! Do you see any gnat shit? You have to get on your knees to see the gnat shit. (*Tyrone hesitates.*) On your knees, boy! (*Tyrone gets on his knees, uneasily.*) Get real close. Closer . . . Close enough to taste it. You know what gnat shit taste

like, son? They made me lick gnat shit from my own headlights. Naomi, Josie, and Little T were forced to watch. And then they made me . . . (*Struggling.*) They made me strip down to my underwear—

TYRONE: Grandpa, don't tell me any more of this.

BIG T: Shut up and listen!

TYRONE: I can't bear it.

BIG T: Boy, you telling me to shut up?

TYRONE: (*Noticing Big T is fighting back tears.*) Go on, tell it, Granddad.

BIG T: (*After a moment, reaching out and embracing Tyrone through tears.*) I love you, Tyrone. Come on. Help me put this car back together.

TYRONE: You got it.

BIG T: It's gonna kill Naomi to see her car scattered all over the roadside.

TYRONE: Naw, man, Grandma will never see Molly like this.

BIG T: God bless you.

TYRONE: I'm going to make this Cadillac fit for a queen. What about the wedding dress? There is no way Grandma hand-stitch another dress in time for Denise's wedding.

BIG T: Nothing is wrong with the dress that can't be taken care of. Naomi is another matter.

Second session of "Alabama" fades in. Lights fade on Big T and Tyrone as they begin working on car.

Scene Eight

Jail. Lights rise. A disoriented Naomi scrubs fiercely at her arms and body. "Alabama" fades to background. Josie enters.

NAOMI: He won't wash off. I can't wash him off.

JOSIE: Mama! What are you doing to yourself?

NAOMI: Washing off Doug Winston.

JOSIE:	Stop it.
NAOMI:	He's not coming off.
JOSIE:	You're rubbing yourself raw. We've got to get out of here.
NAOMI:	No, Josie. I can't let T Baby see me like this. I got to wash him off before T Baby sees me.
JOSIE:	Mama!
NAOMI:	Josie, take me to Big Creek.
JOSIE:	Big Creek? That's in Mississippi, Mama.
NAOMI:	I've got to wash him off. Get me to Big Creek!
JOSIE:	What did she do to you?
NAOMI:	Bumping and grinding up against me.
JOSIE:	She had no business—
NAOMI:	Doug Winston!
JOSIE:	Dear God.
NAOMI:	Talking about how everything I wore drove him crazy. Stuffing my underwear—
JOSIE:	Mama!
NAOMI:	One morning, I'm in the kitchen cooking his breakfast. I look around, and he is just standing there stark naked. His eyes glued to my every move. I keep my eyes on the coffee pot to avoid him. He just stands there—staring. Then he eases up behind me, wraps his arms around me, and begs me to hold him.
JOSIE:	(*Reaching out and holding Naomi.*) It's okay—
NAOMI:	(*Breaking away.*) It's not okay!
JOSIE:	I'm here.
NAOMI:	I try and get away. (*Josie embraces Naomi in a protective hold.*) He turns me around and forces his lips against mine . . . (*Trying to untangle herself from Josie.*) "I can't! Nooo! Don't, Doug. I have to make your coffee." "I'm not letting you go!" "No, please, the madam's going to hear us!"
JOSIE:	Mama! It's me, Josie!
NAOMI:	He held on to me, Josie, held on until he . . . exploded his wad all over my dress! (*As if to clean something too contaminated to touch.*) I ripped my

	clothes off and ran out the house, and I jumped into Big Creek. I tried to wash him off me.
JOSIE:	(*Shaking Naomi.*) Mama, look at me. He's gone. Gone forever!
NAOMI:	What—is that why she couldn't find him?
JOSIE:	Who couldn't find him?
NAOMI:	That police woman! She pried into every cavity in my body looking for Doug Winston.
JOSIE:	Listen to me, Mama. Nobody can find him. He'll never touch you again. I promise. Never again, okay? Repeat after me. "T Baby loves me." Say it. "T Baby loves me!"
NAOMI:	"T Baby loves me."
JOSIE:	I love you. Tyrone loves you. God loves you. Nobody is going to harm you. (*Embracing Naomi.*) Okay?

Naomi and Josie cling to each other in embrace.

NAOMI:	Josie, baby! Thank God for you.
JOSIE:	Let's get out of here. Daddy and Tyrone are waiting.

Betty enters. Josie and Naomi cling to each other.

BETTY:	You folk have to vacate the premises, ma'am. We've got others waiting.
JOSIE:	(*Furious but measured.*) Have you no shame?
BETTY:	Hold your tongue, miss.
JOSIE:	You have a very pleasant day.
BETTY:	I'll do my best, ma'am.

Naomi turns to Betty and speaks with disarming calm etched in pity.

NAOMI:	God loves you too, baby. (*As Betty averts her eyes.*) God loves all of his children.
BETTY:	Good day, ma'am.

Lights down. "Highway to Heaven" fades in.

Scene Nine

Tyrone has reassembled the Cadillac. It is like brand-new—polished, waxed, detailed. He and Big T are elegantly attired in new suits. They give each other a hand with the finishing touches.

TYRONE:	How long would Molly have sat on the blocks if I hadn't taken her off?
BIG T:	Hard to say. I could have gotten a pretty penny for this car. Naomi, she wouldn't let me sell it. She had to have this car for Denise's wedding.
TYRONE:	Face it, Molly couldn't stay on the blocks forever.
BIG T:	I can't deny that. But there's a bigger reason she's off the blocks, a whole world bigger than Denise's wedding.
TYRONE:	Yeah, what?
BIG T:	A man runs and runs from his past. Thinks he's got it beat, whipped real good. By George, he wakes up one morning and there it is, staring him square in the face. Like a long time enemy that's turned into a good neighbor. You come to see that no matter how hard you try, you can't separate the pain from the glory. They come wrapped in the same package. This thing called life is nothing but a never-ending school filled with nonstop lessons twenty-four hours seven days a week. God knows some lessons hurt like the devil in hell, but if they don't kill you, they make you a hell of a lot stronger.
TYRONE:	That which doesn't kill us makes us stronger.
BIG IT:	Yeah, that's the real reason Molly is off the blocks.
TYRONE:	Since the day I first saw Molly, I've wanted to design cars. You think Grandma will be pleased?
BIG T:	Naomi will be pleased. You got the suit to match.
TYRONE:	Me? Look at you. (*Straightening Big T's tie.*) Dressed like a man straight out of *Gentleman's Quarterly*!
BIG T:	When I was a little kid, Mama took empty wheat flour sacks and sewed my school clothes. The other kids poked fun at me. "Here comes flour sack

	Tyrone." I've spent my life running from flour sack clothes.
TYRONE:	Not anymore. Granddad, you look like the groom waiting on his bride.
BIG T:	I *am* the groom. I *am* waiting on my beautiful bride. As for you, look at my handsome best man. You are truly my best man.

Josie and Naomi enter, arm in arm. They are dressed in new outfits, Naomi in a classy white outfit, suggesting life anew.

NAOMI:	T Baby . . .
BIG T:	Mercy! (*Taking Naomi by the hand.*) I'm hearing wedding bells all over.
NAOMI:	T Baby (*blushing helplessly*), you think so?
BIG T:	I *know* so.
NAOMI:	Oh stop it. (*Noticing Molly.*) Goodness, Molly looks brand-new.
BIG T:	Guess who's looking better than Molly? Looking good. She's aging like fine wine. (*To Naomi's delight.*) Smelling good. Let me see how you feel. (*Holding her hand.*) Feeling like brand-new. Mercy!
NAOMI:	You think so?
BIG T:	I know so. (*Embracing Naomi again in secure hug.*) Get yourself in this car before Molly starts screaming and shouting at you for holding up the wedding. (*Stepping back and holding onto Naomi's hands.*)
NAOMI:	T Baby . . .
TYRONE:	No need to say a word. Molly told Tyrone everything—from A to Z. Old gal couldn't stop running her motor mouth.
JOSIE:	Everything, Daddy?
BIG T:	Everything. You folk ought a been there. Did I hear you say something Tyrone?

Tyrone passes gift-wrapped package to Naomi. She opens it and pulls out a wedding tiara. Tyrone places tiara on Naomi's head.

TYRONE:	Queen Naomi.
JOSIE:	Beautiful, Mama.
TYRONE:	Yeah, Grandma, beautiful.

Tyrone pulls bouquet of red roses from back seat and presents them to Naomi. He escorts Naomi to front seat passenger side. Big T embraces Josie. Then they settle into their seats.

BIG T: Josie, I need you to recite that poem for me.

There is a moment of painful silence. Josie struggles to speak.

JOSIE:	I don't know if I remember it.
BIG T:	Just this once.
JOSIE:	Dad . . .
BIG T:	I won't ever ask you again.

Big T seems about to break apart. Tyrone breaks the silence, slowly, resolutely.

TYRONE:

> *And Moses lifted up his rod*
> *Over the Red Sea;*
> *And God with a blast of his nostrils*
> *Blew the waters apart,*
> *And the Children of Israel all crossed over*
> *On to the other side.*

(Tyrone places his arm around Josie.)

JOSIE AND NAOMI:

> *And Moses sang and Miriam danced,*
> *And the people shouted for joy,*
> *And God led the Hebrew Children on*
> *Till they reached the Promised Land.*

BIG T:

> *Listen!—Listen!*
> *All you sons of Pharaoh.*

THE FAMILY:

> *Who do you think can hold God's people*
> *When the Lord God himself has said,*
> *Let my people go?*

(*Big T checks out rearview mirror.*)

BIG T: Well do Jesus. We've got company.

Naomi places her arm around Big T. He reciprocates.

"Highway to Heaven" fades in. The family begins to sing along in joyful defiance.

END OF PLAY

PAUL ROBESON PERFORMING ARTS COMPANY PRODUCTION

Thruway Diaries made its Central New York at the Paul Robeson Performing Arts Company at Syracuse University on October 25, 2008 with the following artists and production staff.

CAST

Big T	Samuel L. Kelley
Naomi	Ms. Blyss
Little T/Tyrone	Ryan Travis
Josie	Jessica Ann Mitchell
Baylor/Whelan/Rock	Bill Lee
Taylor/Dirk/Stick/State Trooper	Mathias Sajovitz
Police Officer Betty	Ann Childress
	Kathy Good
Police Commissioner	Bill Yost

PRODUCTION AND DESIGN

Executive Artistic Director	William H. Rowland II
Associate Artistic Director	Annette Adams-Brown
Director	Samuel L. Kelley
Co-director	Jackie Warren-Moore
Set Designers	Samuel L. Kelley

	Anne Childress
Costume Coordination	Patricia McCullars
Costume Assistants	Venise Toussaint
	Leneika Satchell, Azana Simon, Nico Scott
Sound & Lights	Benjamin Robinson
Sound & Lighting Assistant	Lavar Lobdell
Stage Manager	Anne Childress
	Jon Meldrum, Larry Norton, Kyle Bell
Program Cover Design	Victor Garcia
PowerPoint Presentation	Anne Childress
Power Point Operator	Lavar Lobdell
Set Construction & Theater Prep Crew	Jeff Johns
	Irwin Johnson, Jafon'ta Johnson, Marquis
	"Rocko" Johnson Jeff Johnson, Teondre Johnson

Stage Hands/Crew	Alexandria B. Kimbrough Lavar Lobdell,
	Tucker Baumbach
Ushers	Derrick Reeder, Heath Mills, Kareem Reid
	Al Hoy, Abdul Karim Abdullah, Gianna Gill,
	Eugene Newsome II, Derrell Smith, Kristen Harleston,
	Ayisha Crockrell, Jessica Johnson

As part of the Syracuse University African American Studies Program, the Paul Robeson Performing Arts Company enriched the experiences of students in Professor William Rowland's theater classes through including them in the production process. For this *Thruway Diaries* production, these areas included sound, lighting, costume, power point operations, set construction, and house operations, including ushering.

I am also taken by the outstanding job the actors in this production have displayed during this eight week rehearsal period. Some of them never having been on stage before and others just darn wonderful actors . . . Adam Banks and his sterling community class called Malcolm and Martin: Justice Between the Dream and the Nightmare, has supported wholeheartedly this project in numerous ways. We'd like to thank them all for their support.

—William Rowland II, Executive Artistic Director
Paul Robeson Performing Arts Company

NOTES FROM THE PLAYWRIGHT

The notes below are intended as a guide to assist those producing *Thruway Diaries*.

Production and Design

The set and scene design is meant to be sparse rather than elaborate. Costumes play a significant role in evoking the times. As always, human and financial resources will be the major determining factors.

Police Commissioner

This role was played by an additional actor at the Paul Robeson Performing Arts Company production in Syracuse. The Jubilee Theatre production videotaped one of the police officers, who also doubled as the commissioner. Both worked extremely well. Choose the option that works best for you.

Church Scene

Some theatres do this with still shots on video, while others go live with the family. Keeping it live engages the audience more directly.

Strip Search Scene of the Women

This action has been done behind a screen, with Josie seen from the shoulders up. One production went for the silhouette. Nudity is not recommended, as it calls attention to itself.

Post-Performance Dialogue

Racial profiling is a reality in African American and Latino communities across America. A dialogue following each performance that includes academic and local communities, the local police department, production artists, and staff proved very valuable with the Paul Robeson Performing Arts Company production. It is highly recommended for your production.

MUSIC AND POETRY REFERENCES

Music and poetry references in the play are from the following works:

God's Trombones: Seven Negro Sermons in Verse, with excerpts from "The Creation" and "Let My People Go" by James Weldon Johnson, first published in 1927. Full text may be found at: http://docsouth.unc.edu/southlit/johnson/johnson.html.

"Precious Memories," credited to J. B. F. Wright, is performed by Sister Rosetta Tharpe, from the album *Precious Memories*. Original release date is October 1997 by Savoy records. Audio CD release date is 14 October 1997.

"Walking Up the King's Highway," by Thomas A. Dorsey, performed by Alex Bradford from the album *Precious Lord: The Great Gospel Songs of Thomas A. Dorsey*. Original release date of audio CD is 8 March 1994 by Legacy/Columbia.

"Alabama" is by John Coltrane, from the album *Live at Birdland (1963)*. Audio CD released 5 November 1996 by Grp Records.

"Get Right Church" is from James Cleveland's album *Rev. James Cleveland: Get Right Church*. Audio CD release date is 23 July 2002.

AND THE BEAT GOES ON: RACIAL PROFILING BEFORE AND AFTER 9/11

My Uncle Joe sits in his beat-up Chevy pickup, trembling in fear as the scene before him unfolds. Police officers in Clarksdale, Mississippi, pull over a black man. He is driving a late-model Cadillac, most likely from Chicago, the Promised Land of the black migration arriving from the heart of the Mississippi Delta. The police order the black man out of his car and make him get down on his knees. Then they force him to lick the headlights of his own Cadillac. "I was scared to death," exclaimed Uncle Joe, still recovering from shock as he sat in our kitchen recounting the story to my mother several days later.

This was the early sixties, a time when Northern blacks, sporting the latest model cars and fashions, flaunted their newly minted status as members of the burgeoning black middle class. But boldly displaying such material prosperity was often seen as an affront to southern white dominance and was sometimes met with brutal resistance from law enforcement officials, who were given free rein to harass and abuse without fear of reproach. This was not racial profiling as we have come to know it today. It was a way of life.

Fast-forward to the 1990s. Imagine the young man who was humiliated by the Mississippi police as a senior citizen, the venerated family patriarch, now well into his seventies. He is retired. His Cadillac, which sat on the block for many years because of the shattering impact of the ugly Mississippi incident, has been restored and modernized by his grandson, an automotive engineer with a knack for restoring old cars. The family patriarch, his wife, middle-aged daughter, and grandson take to the road for vacation. What is the world into which they are now driving? A world at the mercy of America's War on Drugs. It is a world in which the United States Supreme Court has validated "stop and frisk" by police, a world in which the court has further ruled that any traffic offense committed by a driver, no matter how minor, is a legitimate legal basis for a stop, a world in which that minor traffic offense forms the basis for the pretext stop, an action that has become the "Bible" for racial profiling in America's War on Drugs. They are driving into a world in which the racialization of cocaine means federal penalties for crack cocaine are a hundred times harsher than those for powder cocaine. And it will remain that way until America's first elected African American president intervenes and changes the rules. They are driving into a world in which the grandson, if convicted of possession of crack cocaine, could experience a "living death" that strips him of his human and civil rights, a world where his future as a first-rate automotive designer could be destroyed. This world is one in which the Drug Policy Alliance claims that the mass criminalization of young African American men is as "profound a system of racial control as the Jim Crow laws" that prevailed in America for a hundred years. It is a world in which the Zero Tolerance policy in schools for black men has resulted in what civil rights lawyer and author Michelle Alexander calls a pipeline that runs from high school to prison.

Yet the black patriarch and his family see themselves as the quintessential American family embarking on their dream vacation. They are living witnesses that much has changed for the better in America. But police officers blinded by racial stereotypes see something strikingly different in the family's vintage Cadillac. They see a vehicle transporting illegal drugs. Hence, zealous officers can't resist ripping apart piece by piece this symbol of African American success in order to find the "true" reason for its existence, anything other than the honest pursuit of the American Dream. In their haste to take this symbol of success apart, the officers make few distinctions between the innocent and the criminal, the elderly and the young, the professional and the blue-collar worker. One need not be caught in the act of committing a criminal offense or appearing suspicious or wearing the trendiest hip-hop clothing and accessories. Being black is more than enough. The action of the police officers presumes guilt by color and association, a form of profiling that came to be known as "driving while black." Put more succinctly, using race as a basis for stopping drivers, or for searches and seizures in the case of Customs, is racial profiling.

While African American and Latino men were most likely to be the targets of searches related to driving and street-level drug searches, a more degrading activity emerged, affecting African American women: flying while black. Returning to the United States from international trips, black women found themselves targets of strip searches by US Customs agents at a disproportionately higher rate than any other racial or gender group. The General Accounting Office (GAO) issued a report in April 2000, noting that black women were nine times more likely to undergo an x-ray for carrying drugs than their white female counterparts, even though black women were not nearly as likely to be found carrying contraband. Black women kept their humiliating experience mainly to themselves until several went public with their stories, detailing their strip search experiences in Chicago in 1998. The floodgates opened with thirteen hundred coming forward to tell their stories in the Chicago area alone. Chicago attorney Richard Fox ended up representing close to ninety black women who filed a class-action lawsuit against the US Customs Service at Chicago's O'Hare International Airport. Profiling tactics used by Customs Services reflected a commonly held stereotype about the black woman—poor, pregnant, and on social services. Black women deviating from this stereotypical norm, such as professional and middle-class women with the financial wherewithal to afford international travel, must be engaged in illegal activity. By virtue of their color, they had been cast as "drug mules," leading Customs to essentially declare black women as guilty before they even left the country, thus all but guaranteeing a strip search on their return.

Small wonder then that a black woman returning home from abroad might find herself, as one woman described her ordeal, in a place that looked like a "South American torture chamber" as she was put through a body search while another would end up on the hospital table with her legs in the stirrups and a doctor probing her insides. At least one was required to remove a bloody tampon from her vagina. Her offense was that she appeared evasive in her response to questions regarding the frequency of her travel even though nothing illegal was found on her person or in her bags. More frightening than the invasive searches for many was the terrifying experience of being cut off from friends and family during the entire search procedure. Like Chicago's O'Hare, the problem of racial profiling was rampant at

Atlanta's Hartsfield-Jackson International according to Cathy Harris, who
blew the whistle on what was happening there. Harris, who worked at
Customs for nineteen years, noted that intrusive strip-searches and invasive
procedures involving African American travelers "included being shackled
to hospital beds, with some procedures lasting up to four days for the sole
purpose of Customs Inspectors collecting overtime money."

Back on the highway, this time the New Jersey Turnpike, where Dr. Elmo
Randolph, a dentist, claimed to have been stopped by police approximately
one hundred times. He was never issued a ticket for being stopped. Even
so, police, according to Dr. Randolph, searched his luxury car, interrogated
him about where he purchased it, and also about his profession. Racial
profiling reached its most notorious level in New Jersey in April 1998 when
state troopers shot and wounded four black and Latino youth riding in a
van. The act of violence against the youth drew national attention from
the media and caused much public outrage within the black community.
Further complicating matters were lawsuits filed against New Jersey State
Police by the American Civil Liberties Union on behalf of Dr. Randolph and
several others. New Jersey entered into an agreement with the US Justice
Department in 1999 to "remedy" racial profiling. As for the shooting of
the four men on the New Jersey Turnpike, the state troopers involved in
the shooting took the fall. Their crime in the final analysis: obstructing
the investigation into the shooting in which they injured the four black
and Latino youth.

By the late 1990s and early 2001, racial profiling had become an undeniable
part of America's national agenda. President George W. Bush declared to a
joint session of Congress on February 27, 2001:   "Racial   profiling
is wrong, and we will end it in America." Georgia congressman John
Lewis, himself an activist during the Civil Rights Movement, and Illinois
senator Richard Durbin each proposed legislation in 2000 and 2001
respectively that sought to prevent Customs from using such factors as race
and religion as the primary indicators for subjecting travelers to intrusive
searches without having the appropriate documentation. Amid the despair
was much hope. The time had finally arrived for the country to develop a
long-term solution to a problem that had reached crisis level for African
Americans.

Then on the morning of Tuesday, September 11, 2001, Islamist terrorists struck the heart of America's financial and military might, destroying New York City's World Trade Center Towers and temporarily crippling the Pentagon in Arlington, Virginia. Nearly three thousand people perished in the attacks, including citizens from close to a hundred countries, with countless others sustaining injuries. The US stock market experienced a financial tsunami to the tune of nearly 1.5 trillion dollars the week the markets reopened, while the searing emotional and psychological scars inflicted on the nation's psyche were incalculable.

With the 9/11 hijackers being identified as Middle Eastern in origin—fifteen from Saudi Arabia alone—suddenly, America's "Wanted Dead or Alive" poster had a new face: Osama bin Laden. Racial profiling quickly expanded beyond blacks and Latinos to include the "Middle Eastern" terrorist. The War on Terror was the new battlefront. The Bush administration and the US Congress responded to the attacks with unprecedented security legislation, creating the Department of Homeland Security and passage of the USA PATRIOT Act. Most significant of all, the Aviation and Transportation Security Act established the Transportation Security Administration (TSA), making the federal government responsible for airport security. The result has been the most intrusive and controversial screening measures for travelers in recorded history and for air travelers in particular.

In theory, every person boarding a plane is a suspect until cleared by security. In reality, however, sweeping security measures have led to profiles that rely on stereotypical demographics—ethnicity, race, religion, and national origin—as the standard for most searches. As Curt Goering, senior deputy executive director of Amnesty International USA, puts it: "Now,   the practice can be more accurately characterized as driving, flying, walking, worshipping, shopping or staying at home while black, brown, red, yellow, Muslim or of Middle-Eastern appearance." According to Amnesty International, racial profiling "directly affects Native Americans, Asian Americans, Hispanic Americans, African Americans, Arab Americans, Persian Americans, American Muslims, many immigrants and visitors, and, under certain circumstances, white Americans." It notes that the number of Americans reporting that they have been profiled by race is thirty-two million, roughly the population of the Commonwealth of Canada. Recent complaints against the New York City Police Department's profiling of Muslims have not found widespread support, in that most of those polled overwhelmingly support New York Police Chief Raymond Kelly on the issue. Seemingly forgotten in the wake of this expanded profiling is the fact that some of the most violent deaths in America have come from white homegrown terrorists who hide safely within their own culture and thereby comfortably avoid the disturbing and suspicious gaze rendered through racial profiling.

Let us presume that the young man who was forced down on his knees to lick the grit and grime from his own Cadillac in Mississippi in the early sixties is headed home for his annual Juneteenth family reunion for one last time. He is now well into his eighties but in generally good health for a man of his years. Wary of the discomfort that comes with cramping his infirm body into a car for eight to ten hours, he reluctantly agrees to make the trip by plane. At the airport, it is likely he will be screened using advanced imaging technology, perhaps a backscatter x-ray body scanner that will render a "virtual" strip search of his body. He will leave it to privileged whites with time and money on their hands to duke it out with TSA over Fourth Amendment rights. For these rights have come to mean very little to him in a nation where his rights have been systematically stripped by a judicial process that has all but reinstituted a Jim Crow society disguised as the new Color Blind America. Nor will he meet the latest TSA "PreCheck" program qualifications that expedite screening for a cost of one hundred dollars. It is by invitation only to frequent flyers. He does meet the newly instituted modified TSA procedures for senior citizens over seventy-five, but it is only in the test stages and not at his security checkpoint.

He is, however, acquainted with x-ray imaging and is suspicious of its potentially damaging effects on the body. He hesitates at the point of screening, thinking of his pacemaker, fearing a human error or technical glitch in that brief moment during which he will be subjected to the scanner could mean never seeing his family again. Taking no chances, he offers his pacemaker card and requests a private screening. His pacemaker card, not to mention his age, should be his passport to the plane. But his actions trigger something in the officious TSA agent's mind: This old black guy could very well be the next "underwear bomber" in the manner of Nigerian Islamist Umar Farouk Abdulmutallab, who tried to destroy a plane using explosives hidden in his underwear. A ridiculous thought even to the TSA agent, but he takes no chances.

The elderly black man is taken into a private room. The agent dons gloves and proceeds to run his hand over the gentleman's groin, inner thigh, and over what the passenger will later recall to family and friends as his "manhood." He is more relieved than humiliated when the "sexual assault" is over. God forbid he should scream: "I've been stripped searched!" There would be no US and state senators rushing to his aid, demanding that TSA provide advocates for people like him. Nor is it highly likely that his story would go viral on the world wide web or become the salacious subject of TV talk shows and news programs where tens of millions could watch—with curious amusement, or with outrage and disgust. He is an old black man making his way through a security system that treats him as a slow moving number holding up an otherwise efficient TSA security process.

Finally, he arrives at his destination. There, he is greeted and embraced as the revered family patriarch who has triumphed against the odds. He will disclose his latest experience of racial profiling, of being probed and poked, with amusement etched in caustic wit. But he will do so in the company of those who love and admire him for his wit and wisdom, most likely over his favorite comfort food, fresh baked sweet potato pie and barbecue chicken. Love of family trumps the pain of that humiliating experience so many years ago as well as the latest indignity that he and so many like him have endured and will continue to endure with the certainty of the rising and setting of the sun.

Samuel L. Kelley
October 1, 2012

SELECTED BIBLIOGRAPHY

The publications selected below are recommended for additional reading. They were helpful in preparing this article, which grew out of a seminar presented in February 2012 at the State University of New York College at Cortland titled "Drop Your Pants and Bend Over: Racial Profiling Before and After 9/11."

Democratic Warriors .com. "Racial-Profiling-Since-9-11Increased." 14 November 2006. Accessed: 24 January 2012. http://www. democraticwarrior.com/forum/showthread.php?6302-Racial-Profiling-Since-9-11-Increased

Drug Policy Alliance. "Race And The Drug War." 2012 Accessed: 23 January 2012. http://www.drugpolicy.org/issues/race-and-drug-war/our-priorities

Durbin, Richard, Senator. Reasonable Search Standards Act. (introduced 4/30/2001). Accessed: 7 March 2012. < http://thomas.loc.gov/cgi-bin/query/z?c107:S.799:>

Fox, Edward M. Hearing on the U.S. Customs Service Passenger Inspection Operations. "Statement of Edward M. Fox, Esq., Ed Fox & Associates, Chicago, Illinois." Testimony Before the Subcommittee on Oversight, of the House Committee on Ways and Means. 20 May 1999. Accessed: 20 January 2012. <http://waysandmeans.house.gov/legacy/oversite/106cog/5-20-99/5-20fox.htm>

Lobe, Jim. Anti War.com. "Amnesty Intl.: Racial Profiling Much Worse Since 9/11." 14 September 2004. Accessed: 24 January 2012. <http:// www.antiwar.com/lobe/?articleid=3571> Goering, Kurt

Lewis, John, Representative. Civil Rights for International Travelers Act. (introduced 5/24/2001) 6/4/2001 Referred to House subcommittee. Status: Referred to the Subcommittee on Trade. Accessed: 7 March 2012. http://thomas.loc.gov/cgi-bin/bdquery/?&Db=d107&querybd=@ FIELD(FLD001+@4 (Sexual+orientation))

Sokolower, Jody. Rethinking Schools Blog. "Michelle Alexander on The New Jim Crow and the school-to-prison pipeline." 20 December 2011. Accessed: 26 January 2012. http://rethinkingschoolsblog.wordpress. com/2011/12/20/michelle-alexander-on-the-new-jim-crow-and-the-school-to-prison-pipeline/

Sugrue, Thomas J. Automobile in Life and Society in America. "Driving While Black: The Car and Race Relations in America." Accessed: 23 August 2012. http://www.autolife.umd.umich.edu/Race/R_ Casestudy/R_Casestudy.htm

United States General Accounting Office. Report to the Honorable Richard J. Durbin, United States Senate. U. S. Customs Service. "Better Targeting of Airline Passengers for Personal Searches Could Produce Better Results." March 2000. Accessed: 7 March 2012. http://www. gao.gov/new.items/gg00038.pdf

ABOUT THE PLAYWRIGHT

Sam Kelley first came to the attention of the theatre community with the production of his critically acclaimed play *Pill Hill*, which premiered at the Yale Repertory Theatre when he was a playwriting student at the Yale School of Drama. *Pill Hill* has since been produced in theatres around the country, including the Hartford Stage, Philadelphia Theatre Company, Chicago Theatre Company, ETA Creative Arts Foundation, Chicago, Ensemble Theatre in Houston, Penumbra Theatre Company, St. Paul, Minnesota, Florida A & M University, Tallahassee, North Carolina A & T University, Raleigh, Coppin State University, Baltimore, Maryland, and the University of Arkansas at Pine Bluff, to name a few. In addition to its St. Paul production, Penumbra Theatre Company presented *Pill Hill* at the National Black Theatre Festival in Winston-Salem, North Carolina. Among the theaters that have won awards for their productions of *Pill Hill* are the Chicago Theatre Company *(*Joseph Jefferson Award for Best Ensemble Performance*)*, ETA Creative Arts Foundation *(*Black Theatre Alliance Awards for Best Costume Design, Best Ensemble, Best Performance in an Ensemble—Actor, and Best Direction*)*, Karamu Theatre, Cleveland, Ohio *(*Kieffer Award for Best Production*)*, and New Horizons Theatre, Pittsburgh (Onyx Awards for Best Ensemble Performance, Lead Actor, and Lighting).

Staged readings and productions of Kelley's works have been presented at such places as Jubilee Theatre in Fort Worth, Texas *(Thruway Diaries)*, Plowshares Theatre, Detroit, Michigan *(White Chocolate)*, Billie Holiday Theatre in New York City *(White Chocolate)*, Juneteenth Legacy Theatre, Louisville, Kentucky *(Faith Hope and Charity: The Story of Mary McLeod Bethune, Habeas Corpus, Driving While Black,* and *Ain't Got Time To Die)*,

African American Theatre Program at the University of Louisville *(Thruway Diaries* and *Blue Vein Society)*, Claflin University *(Driving While Black)*, Paul Robeson Performing Arts Company, Syracuse, New York *(The Blue Vein Society, Thruway Diaries,* and others), Wales, United Kingdom, University of Glamorgan at Pontypridd at the Theatres of Science Conference *(A Hero For McBride)*, Center for the Arts, Homer, New York *(Beautiful Game)*, and *(Faith, Hope and Charity: The Story of Mary McLeod Bethune,)* Christ Community Church, Cortland, New York.

Penumbra Theatre Company awarded Kelley the Cornerstone Competition playwriting award and the Yale School of Drama the Molly Kuhn Award for *PILL HILL*. Kelley is the recipient of the *James Thurber Playwright-In-Residence* award from the Thurber House in Columbus, Ohio, which was awarded during the spring of 1998. During that time, Kelley also served as playwright-in-residence at Ohio State University. Additional residencies include the Blue Mountain Center in Blue Mountain Lakes, New York, the Virginia Center for the Creative Arts in Mt. San Angelo, Virginia, Byrdcliffe Arts Colony in Woodstock, New York, Mary Anderson Center for the Arts in Mt. St. Francis, Indiana, and Yaddo in Saratoga Springs, New York.

Pill Hill was published by Dramatic Publications in 1995 and also anthologized in <u>New American Plays</u>, Heinemann Books, 1992. Two *Pill Hill* scenes appeared in <u>Best Monologues for Male Actors</u>, 1992. Kelley's article, *"Playwright gives crux of Pill Hill,"* appeared in the *Philadelphia Inquirer,* January, 29, 1992, while another article, "Sidney Poitier: heros integrationniste," appeared in *Cinemaction,* Paris, France, 1988.

In addition to his work as a playwright, Kelley has performed at the school and community levels for most of his life. His first and second grade teachers put him on the stage and he has been there, more or less, ever since. However it was during the eighth grade that Kelley first performed James Weldon Johnson's "The Creation" from Johnson's book of sermon poems *God's Trombones* at the St. Luke Missionary Baptist Church in Turkey Scratch, Arkansas. Today, Kelley is known in the Cortland area for his performances of the works of Johnson and Martin Luther King, Jr. He has performed *I Have A Dream, I've Been to the Mountain Top,* and *Letter from the Birmingham Jail* for more than thirty years.

Kelley is teaches Communication Studies and Africana Studies at the State University of New York (SUNY) College at Cortland where his favorite courses include Films of Spike Lee, African Americans in TV and Film, Human Communication, and Interviewing Principles and Practices. He has also taught a number of special topics courses, such as African American Women in Theatre, African American Theatre and Video Workshop, Screen writing and Films of Spike Lee for Teachers.

The Board of Trustees of the State University of New York promoted Kelley to the rank of Distinguished Service Professor in 2008 for his many years of outstanding service. He is also the recipient of the SUNY Chancellor's Award for Excellence in Research and Creative Activities. Kelley has served as the Honors Convocation Keynote Speaker and was the SUNY Cortland President's Scholars Inaugural Reception Keynote Speaker. Among other noted awards are the SUNY Cortland Dedicated Service Award, Africana Studies Department, the 25th Anniversary Award for distinguished service and dedication to the SUNY Cortland Gospel Choir, Office of Multicultural Life Unity Celebration Award, Cortland Educational Opportunity Program (EOP) Special Appreciation Award presented by the staff and students of the EOP Program, and the Tompkins Community College Appreciation Award from the Black Student Union.

Kelley received his PhD in Speech, with a concentration in Radio-TV-Film, from the University Michigan and his MFA in playwriting from the Yale School of Drama. He earned his MA in Speech from Arkansas at Fayetteville and his BA in Speech and Drama from Arkansas at Pine Bluff. He has also studied screen writing, playwriting and Film Script development at New York University. A graduate of M. M. Tate High School in Marvell, Kelley claims Turkey Scratch, Arkansas as home.

Current professional memberships include Dramatists Guild of America, Black Theatre Network, United University Professions, and Phi Kappa Phi National Honor Society.